"It's an... Samantha, isn't it?

She grew still in Jason's arms but he didn't release her. She could feel his warm breath against her cheek, see the pulse at the base of his throat. Her own pulse began to beat. "Isn't it?" he asked again.

"Please—"

"Please?" His mouth curved into a smile. "Why, thank you. Don't mind if I do. I thought you'd never ask."

Then his lips closed over hers.

This kiss was nothing like the smacking one he'd given her in the restaurant or the fleeting brush of his lips at the airport. The sheer shock of it took her breath away, set her heart into a frantic staccato beat. It was everything she'd ever imagined a kiss could be and until now, had never known. It was sweetness, warmth, desire and passion....

American author **ANNE McALLISTER** majored in Spanish
literature, has a master's degree in theology, copyedited
textbooks and ghostwrote sermons. She might never
have pursued her earlier interest in writing if a friend
hadn't challenged her to write a Harlequin Romance. She
has successfully met the challenge with many popular
novels in Harlequin's Romance, Presents and American
lines. She regards herself as blessed with a "terrifically
tolerant husband" and "four opinionated but equally
supportive children." In all her stories she writes about
relationships—how they grow and how they challenge
the people who share them.

Books by Anne McAllister

HARLEQUIN PRESENTS
844—LIGHTNING STORM
1060—TO TAME A WOLF
1099—THE MARRIAGE TRAP
1257—ONCE A HERO

HARLEQUIN ROMANCE
2721—DARE TO TRUST

HARLEQUIN AMERICAN ROMANCE
186—BODY AND SOUL *
202—DREAM CHASERS
234—MARRY SUNSHINE
275—GIFTS OF THE SPIRIT
309—SAVING GRACE
341—IMAGINE
387—I THEE WED

*THE QUICKSILVER SERIES

ANNE MCALLISTER

out of bounds

Harlequin Books

TORONTO • NEW YORK • LONDON
AMSTERDAM • PARIS • SYDNEY • HAMBURG
STOCKHOLM • ATHENS • TOKYO • MILAN

For Ray Olivere,
an artist and a gentleman,
with gratitude and admiration
for his many wonderful covers

Harlequin Presents first edition June 1991
ISBN 0-373-11371-4

Original hardcover edition published in 1990
by Mills & Boon Limited

OUT OF BOUNDS

CHAPTER ONE

'No.' SAMANTHA knotted her fingers together in her lap and lifted her gaze to meet the steely blue eyes that bored into her own. She thrust out her chin. 'No—thank you very much, but I'm afraid I shall have to decline.'

'No?' The man echoed the word as if it were unknown to him. Indeed Samantha suspected it might have been. She doubted if people said it very often to Jason Cole.

'But you haven't even asked any questions,' he said.

'I know enough.' She shook her head again resolutely. 'No, thank you. I'm sorry.'

She wasn't. The last thing on earth she wanted was to spend a summer in this man's employ, even if the employment was teaching cello and chaperoning his very talented fifteen-year-old sister. Once she had heard that they would be spending the summer living with him, she'd made up her mind. There was no way Samantha wanted to do that.

She might have only met him ten minutes earlier, but she'd needed scarcely ten seconds to know he was everything she detested in a man!

Samantha had no use at all for arrogant, high-powered businessmen, especially ones as drop-dead handsome as this one. She knew the dangers of them, particularly ones who could make you forget your name and all your common sense with a single look. And it had taken her only one and she'd known Jason Cole could do just that.

Her first glimpse of him standing at the bay window of the Rudley School's proper front parlour had made her palms damp, her mouth dry, and her heart beat as

5

if it, not the jackhammer three doors down on Columbus Avenue, had been making that ungodly noise.

It was exactly the sort of intense physical reaction that her father had always warned her against. 'Hormones!' Ambrose Peabody had snorted. 'Foolishness! You know what happens!'

Samantha did—the sort of thing her mother had done when confronted by Louis Lambert, the sort of thing she herself had once done when faced with the suave, sophisticated Fritz. But Fritz had been a lesson well learned.

'Don't worry,' she'd always replied. 'It'll never happen again.'

But now it had.

She'd been tempted to turn and run. Instead she'd simply sat down opposite him, steeled herself against the man and his charm. Whatever he wanted, she wasn't doing it. And that was that. She swallowed hard and licked her lips.

'Not enough money?' He didn't seem to be taking her 'no' all that seriously.

He was lounging in one of the high-backed wing-chairs, one long leg crossed over the other at the knee. He wore a dark grey three-piece suit that looked as if it had been tailored to fit his particular muscles. And his strong jaw and long, slightly crooked nose added an unmistakable authority to the power lent him by his clothes. She thought he was in his early thirties, but they had clearly been hard years. His handsome face was tanned and weather-beaten, somewhat incongruous with the tailored suit. But the incongruity only added to the image of lightly leashed power.

She felt like a mouse tossed into the cage with a lion, one who was trying to make up his mind whether or not he was hungry.

Jason Cole was regarding her with tolerant, amused interest, one corner of his wide mouth lifted. 'So name your price.'

Samantha sucked in her breath. 'I don't *have* a price, Mr Cole. Besides,' she added for good measure, 'I already have a job.'

One dark eyebrow lifted. 'Beasley didn't mention one.'

Beasley, the Rudley School headmaster, didn't know. It was not official yet. But Samantha wasn't saying that.

'I—I am expecting to play in a chamber group this summer.'

'What chamber group?'

'For a concert tour. I'm going to be part of a group, accompanying my——' Samantha faltered here. She wanted to say 'fiancé', but she and Oliver hadn't quite made it to that stage yet. Still, it was only a matter of time. '—my boyfriend,' she compromised.

'Your boyfriend?' Once more the eyebrow lifted as if the possibility of Samantha's having a boyfriend hadn't occurred to him. His scrutiny deepened. She'd often read that men could undress women with their eyes, but she'd never experienced it herself. Until now.

Bristling, she stood up, felt even more exposed to his gaze, and promptly sat right back down again. 'Yes. My boyfriend. Oliver Archer.' She gave him a significant look. Take that, she thought.

Jason Cole looked totally blank.

'Oliver Archer,' Samantha repeated. 'The flautist.' Hadn't the man even heard of him, for goodness' sake?

Jason rolled his eyes. 'A flautist? It figures.'

'He's one of the finest musical talents of this generation!'

'Oh, yes?' He did little to mask the boredom of his words.

'Yes,' Samantha hissed vehemently. 'He's incredibly talented. Sensitive. Passionate.'

'What does he see in you?'

The words hit Samantha like a wet fish across the face. She stared at him, steaming, green eyes flashing fire.

He grinned then and gave her an insolent wink. 'Don't tell me. I can guess.'

Samantha jerked to her feet again.

'Settle down, Ms Peabody,' he said, looking up at her with amusement. 'I just wanted to see if there was more to you than obstinacy.'

'What there is "to me" is none of your business, Mr Cole.'

He ran a hand through thick, razor-cut, straight brown hair. The sun-bleached ends gleamed like gold leaf in the late afternoon sun. Samantha found herself beset by an itch to touch them. She twisted her fingers together tightly in front of her.

Jason Cole sighed. 'No way I can convince you?'

'No.'

'Not even for Andrea?'

'No.' Though it wasn't as easy as she was trying to make it sound. Teaching Andrea Cole was a terrible temptation. Being offered a whole summer to do nothing but concentrate on teaching and chaperoning her prize pupil was almost too good an offer to refuse. If Jason Cole, as his sister's guardian, hadn't been part of the package, she might easily have done it.

As it was, there wasn't a chance.

If she'd at first surmised that Jason was far too much like Lambert, her mother's husband—polished, arrogant, determined, sexy—he'd only just finished confirming it. He was a man who got what he wanted—the way Lambert had got Samantha's mother.

Jason and Lambert even worked in the same business. Oh, granted, Lambert was in Paris, one of the great gurus of high fashion. But Jason Cole was president of Cole Sportswear, one of the brash young upstarts who were revolutionising the leisurewear market throughout the world. While not a guru, perhaps, he was not to be sneezed at, either.

Clothes were clothes, after all. And men—especially hotshot businessmen—were men. There was no way she wanted anything—even peripherally—to do with a man like that. Especially given the reactions he evoked in her.

If Oliver's grant didn't come through, she would stay here. Spending the summer on New York's Upper West Side wouldn't be a picnic. But it would be better than the alternative.

There was silence in the room. Outside, over the hum of heavy afternoon traffic, Samantha could hear the shriek of a siren, the jarring jackhammer. A thin line of perspiration trickled down her back. It was only mid-May and already the temperatures had begun to soar.

Jason Cole drummed his fingers on the arm of the chair, clearly stymied. Whatever he had expected from Samantha Peabody, rejection obviously wasn't it. He regarded her again for a long moment, his gaze inscrutable. Samantha met it unflinchingly.

'So, that's it, then?'

Samantha gave him a thin smile, masking her relief that the interview was ending. 'That's it.'

He shrugged his shoulders, powerful muscles moving smoothly inside the confines of his suit jacket. Then he got to his feet and stood staring down at her. 'It's been...interesting, Ms Peabody,' he drawled at last. 'Andrea spoke highly of you.' Unspoken were the words, 'I can't imagine why,' but Samantha had no trouble hearing them.

He offered her his hand.

She hesitated a moment before taking it. It was a strong hand, tanned and capable with long, square-tipped, short-nailed fingers. He should play the piano, she thought irrelevantly. Reluctantly she placed her own in it. His grasp was warm and dry and yet vibrantly alive against her own. Exactly the way she'd feared it would be. She pulled back at once.

He gave her a sardonic, almost mocking smile. 'If you have a "change of heart", do let me know.'

'Of course,' Samantha lied.

He gave her a long look, then a brief nod. 'Good afternoon, Ms Peabody.' He strode to the door and shut it behind him without a backward glance.

It was a full thirty seconds before Samantha allowed herself to breathe again.

The buzzer to her fourth floor apartment rarely rang. Most of Samantha's friends worked right at Rudley and lived in one of its three attached brownstones, just as she did. But occasionally one of the students called or, sometimes, a parent. Still, Samantha found it surprising whenever it was for her. She turned on the intercom.

'Who is it?'

'It's me,' a masculine voice said.

Samantha's heart skipped a beat. 'Oliver! Come up!'

She flew to the door in joyous anticipation. Oliver spent most of the time in Boston these days. He only got to New York when he was giving a concert or came in for a master's workshop. Ordinarily he called first. An impromptu visit was extremely rare and certainly more than she'd hoped for. She shifted eagerly from one foot to another as she waited for him to climb the four flights of stairs, and she threw her arms around him the moment he arrived.

Oliver bore her hug stolidly, then set her aside and sat down on her lumpy sofa, carefully avoiding the worst of the bulges. He smiled at her as he did so, then held out his hand and pulled her on to his lap.

Samantha felt her heart flutter again, and wondered if perhaps the words she had almost spoken to Jason Cole two days before were about to come true.

She had known Oliver for seven years. He had come to see her father when he had been starting at Juilliard. Though Ambrose Peabody was a violinist, not a flautist, he was still the patron and mentor of the best of America's young soloists. At twenty Oliver had hoped to be counted among them. It wasn't long before Ambrose had deemed that he was. Oliver had been held up to Samantha as the ideal young musician ever since. He was also held up by her father as the ideal young husband.

Samantha knew that Ambrose eagerly anticipated the day that she and Oliver tied the knot, and she was very nearly as eager. Oliver was the man of her dreams.

He was everything she wanted in a man: tall, fair, almost more beautiful than handsome. But more than that he possessed an incredible musical sensitivity. Oliver was a man just like her father. *Not* a man like that blatantly masculine Neanderthal Jason Cole.

Samantha understood Oliver perfectly—his temperament, his idiosyncrasies, his passion, his intelligence. And she'd felt privileged the last four years that he had chosen her to be his girlfriend, that she was the one to whom he brought his problems and his triumphs.

What had brought him here tonight?

A ring, perhaps? They'd been a couple since she had been twenty and he twenty-three. Now, at twenty-four, she was finished with her master's degree and was capable of being the nurturing, supportive wife he needed. And, at twenty-seven, Oliver was beginning to establish an international reputation.

Samantha knew he'd been working up to asking her for quite a while, dropping hints, talking about long-term relationships with her family, with what the future would hold for them all. It seemed a good time. She smiled.

Oliver smiled his angelic smile now, too. 'I bring news.'

Samantha waited expectantly, her breath bated.

Suddenly he frowned. 'We need some espresso. Where's the espresso, Sammie? Haven't you got any?'

'Oh, of course.' She jumped up at once. Samantha rarely drank espresso herself, but she kept it on hand for him, the same way she kept a bottle of Seagram's for her father. Now she hurried to the tiny kitchen, calling back out through the door, 'Come out here and tell me.'

'I'll wait.' Oliver sank back on the sofa. 'This is important news. It should be delivered properly.'

So Samantha had to wait until the espresso was ready, and, when it finally was, she poured him a cup and carried it in. Oliver took it without comment, sipped it, then settled back once more.

Samantha perched on a lump next to him.

He turned to her so that she looked directly into his beautiful blue eyes. 'I got the grant.'

Samantha's eyes widened. 'Oh, Oliver! The Fitchton grant?'

Oliver's smile became even more satisfied. 'That's right.'

'But that's wonderful. That means...' Samantha felt her heart nearly bursting. A whole summer travelling with Oliver, playing with Oliver, sharing with Oliver!

'Seven concert weekends,' Oliver said. 'All up and down the East Coast. At all the big summer resorts and cultural meccas. On the Cape. In the Hamptons. Asheville. Williamsburg. You name it.'

'Oh, Oliver, I'm so pleased. You deserve it. Truly you do.'

'I know,' he said simply. He took another swallow of his coffee.

It would be a terrific honeymoon, a concert tour like that. 'Don't you have anything else to tell me?' she asked.

Oliver paused, frowning slightly, then brightened. 'Oh, yes. I've already contacted the back-up people.'

Samantha sighed. No ring tonight. But at least they'd be together. 'Who did you get?' she asked.

'Carlos Andrade's agreed to come as the pianist, and Leopold Kaiser and Jenna Holscher will be the violinists. I talked to Marlin Devane. You know, the violist? He thinks he might be able to clear his schedule and come, too.'

'A terrific group.' Samantha's smile grew. She leaned forward in anticipation. 'And the cellist,' she prompted, smiling, waiting, knowing he'd saved the best for last. 'What about the cellist?'

Oliver shrugged. 'Oh, I asked Nell Strickland.'

'Nell Strickland?'

'Sure. You remember her. Tall gal with flaming red hair. Big—er—boo...breasts. And her ears stick out.'

Her B flats did, too, Samantha thought irritably. Nell Strickland? Curvaceous, simpering, marginally competent Nell? Samantha knew she wasn't in Oliver's league herself, but at least she played in tune! Surely Oliver meant it as a joke. But, just as surely, she knew he didn't. Oliver Archer was not a joking man.

'But why?' she asked, barely able to make it not sound like a wail.

Oliver looked surprised at the question. 'Why not?'

'But I—I'd hoped I——'

Oliver laughed, comprehending suddenly. 'Oh, I couldn't ask *you*.' He reached for her hand and pulled her over into his lap again. '*You* distract me.' And, before Samantha could say a word, his mouth closed over hers, and he was kissing her with persuasive skill.

Off balance, she grabbed for his shoulders, then, persuaded, she began to melt against him, to open her mouth to the pressure of his.

All at once, just as suddenly as he had begun kissing her, Oliver set her aside. 'See what I mean?'

'But——'

He just shook his head and smiled his angel's smile, touching a finger to the tip of her nose. 'Think, Sammie. How could I ever concentrate if you were with me every waking moment?'

Samantha thought it sounded like heaven. But she wasn't proof against the notion that he found her distracting either. It meant that she mattered to him. Her pique lessened, but her disappointment didn't vanish altogether. She couldn't quite banish her scowl.

Oliver grinned at her. 'Don't worry. You'll find something. You're a survivor, Sammie Cat. You always land on your feet.'

Samantha wrinkled her nose at the nickname.

'So cute.' Oliver leaned forward to drop a light kiss on her nose before he pressed his empty espresso cup into her hands and stood up. 'Got to be going. Just thought I'd drop by and tell you the good news.' He paused, looking at her expectantly.

Samantha knew what he expected—the same thing her father always expected—recognition, adulation, praise. And he deserved it, of course, just as her father did.

She smiled at him and gave him another hug, not as enthusiastic a one as she'd have given him if he'd invited her to come along, but a hug none the less.

'Congratulations, Oliver,' she said sincerely. 'I'm sure you'll have a wonderful time.'

'I'm sure I will, too,' he agreed as he touched a strand of her long brown hair. 'And if you really are stuck in the city all summer, maybe I could send you a ticket or two and you could come out to the Hamptons the weekend of the concert.'

Samantha mustered a smile. 'That would be lovely.'

'Front row, centre,' Oliver promised as he walked to the door. He gave her a wink. 'For my girl.'

'This summer?' Cecil Beasley, the Rudley School headmaster, looked at Samantha askance. 'But, my dear Ms

Peabody, I had no idea. I thought...I mean, I understood...I mean, surely, you took...well, I did think...'

Samantha waited for him to explain exactly what it was he did think. Whatever it was, she had the foreboding impression that it wasn't what she hoped it would be.

She sat very quietly in the same wing-chair in which Jason Cole had sat three days before, and waited for Mr Beasley to explain himself.

'I gave the job to Mrs Lamont's nephew,' he said at last, and bent a paper-clip in half.

Samantha simply stared.

Beasley dropped the pieces of paper-clip on the desk, loosened his collar a fraction, then gave her a tight, slightly apprehensive smile. 'When Mr Cole came, I just naturally assumed...' He looked at her hopefully.

'You just naturally assumed what?'

'Why, that you'd taken the job teaching Andrea, of course. She is, after all, your finest student. I couldn't imagine you'd turn it down.'

'I turned it down.'

'But...'

Samantha waited for him to say he understood, that, of course, he'd call bountiful benefactor Gloria Lamont and tell her that her tone-deaf nephew was simply not going to be able to teach strings at Rudley this summer session, that Ms Peabody was going to stay.

He said, easing his collar even looser, 'Well, you understand, I'm sure, my dear. I simply can't just call Mrs Lamont and tell her that Morton won't be needed. I mean, the wiring...the new encyclopaedias...the Lamont scholarship fund...'. He gave Samantha another smile, this one conspiratorial. 'The good of the school, you know.'

Samantha gave him a black look.

'We will, of course, be needing you again in the autumn,' Mr Beasley hastened to assure her. 'Morton is only on holiday from university for the summer term.'

Samantha didn't say anything. She thought of several things she'd have liked to have said. Firstly that, the good lord and Oliver willing, she wouldn't be around in autumn needing a job; second, that she wouldn't take it even if she were; third, that Cecil Beasley was a spineless sponge of a man and she had no respect for him at all.

So she would go home. She might not earn any money that way, but Ambrose would be glad to see her. He would welcome her with open arms to his summer hideaway in the Catskills. It had been just the two of them against the world since her mother had run off with Lambert when Samantha had been only eight years old.

Another father might have left her with a nanny and gone concertising all over the world without her. Ambrose had taken her along. He'd had plans for her. She had been his protégé. All the interest he could spare from his career as an internationally renowned violinist he had invested in her.

Not a violinist like her father because, as he'd often said, 'the comparison would scarcely be fair', Samantha had begun cello at the age of four. He had taught her himself until she had been ten. Then he had found her the best teachers available.

No expense had been spared, no effort left unmade. If sheer love and determination could have made Samantha a virtuoso, she'd have been another Yo Yo Ma. As it was, she was an accomplished cellist—and a disappointment.

Ambrose never said so, of course. He was the best father in the world. But really, Samantha often thought, how could he not be disappointed in her? He had tried so hard, given it everything he had, and still Samantha had failed to live up to his dreams for her.

Poor, dear Ambrose. Talented beyond measure, gifted beyond compare, and always, it seemed to Samantha, shortchanged by life.

First, of course, there had been her mother's betrayal. Ambrose had taken her to Paris while he'd performed in a concert, and there Margot had met Louis Lambert. Instead of focusing entirely on her husband, nurturing and sustaining his marvellous talent and his demanding career, she had let the rising young fashion mogul turn her head.

She had, in fact, let him tempt her, seduce her, and ultimately take her away. In a whirlwind affair that had left international music gossips gasping for breath, she had left Ambrose Peabody and had married Lambert.

Ambrose Peabody—the best, the kindest, the most talented of men—had not deserved such a defection. He deserved love and gratitude and loyalty. He deserved the best. And, from the time she had been eight, Samantha had tried to give it to him.

If Margot wasn't going to be the wife he had hoped for, at least Samantha tried to become the daughter he had wanted her to become. But, however hard she'd tried, she'd never been able to become the cellist of his dreams.

'No matter,' Ambrose had told her when her failure to reach that stature had become all too obvious. He had smiled at her, had put an arm around her shoulders, had given her a squeeze. 'It is not the only vocation, my sweet. To perform is wonderful, but to support performance is also great. Artistry requires such support. It is necessary. You can do that, you know.' He'd got a faraway look in his eyes and then he'd said, with faint bitterness, 'The way your mother never did.'

Samantha understood. She had been relieved. He had been giving her another chance.

First, of course, she'd done it for her father. But, when Oliver had begun to hang around her, talking and smiling, ingratiating himself, she'd found a new focus—a new vocation. Ambrose had been pleased.

He'd encouraged it. It hadn't been long before she and Oliver had become a pair. Samantha understood Oliver. She saw in him the same excess of talent, often misunderstood, that she saw in her father. Maybe her mother had failed her father, but she wouldn't fail Oliver. In that way, perhaps, she'd vindicate one woman, at least, in her father's eyes.

She knew her father would be disappointed that she wasn't joining Oliver this summer. She didn't know quite how, without sounding once more a failure, to tell him that she was coming home instead.

'I'm going to China,' was the first thing he said when she called the next day.

'China?'

'Ten weeks. Isn't it marvellous? Anita has arranged it. A cultural exchange. Concerts in all the major cities. A tremendous opportunity. Simply fantastic. I'm leaving first week in June. Won't be back until mid-August for the Hamptons concert. That's arranged, of course. But until then...' Samantha could almost hear him rubbing his palms together in anticipation. He sounded enormously pleased.

Samantha was stunned. 'How nice,' she managed finally. Perhaps he'd take her along to help manage the trip. She'd done it before.

'Anita's coming, too,' he added. 'She's quite the manager.'

'Quite,' she agreed hollowly. So much for that.

'I'm looking forward to it, I can tell you. We're doing the Brahms with the Beijing Symphony. And the Liszt in Shanghai. And... But what about you, Samantha? What've you and Oliver got planned?'

Samantha swallowed. 'Well,' she said slowly, 'Oliver got the Fitchton grant, so he's going to be doing the concert series.'

'Oh, you'll enjoy that.'

'I—I'm not going.'

'Not going?'

'Well, he asked Nell Strickland to play cello and...'

'Oh, my dear.' Samantha could almost hear her father's frown, his concern. His pity.

'It's all right with me,' she said quickly.

She didn't want his pity, didn't want him feeling sorry for her, feeling she'd failed yet again and that he had to pick up the pieces, say, 'There, there, dear,' and make the best of things for her.

'We're still on, Oliver and I. We just decided that being together all summer was too much of a good thing.'

'Oh?'

'Oh, yes,' Samantha said firmly. 'Hard to concentrate. We'd distract one another, you know.'

'Mmm.' He paused. 'Well, my dear, I'm sure I can find you something.' He sounded tired.

'Not necessary,' Samantha said swiftly. 'I've found my own job.'

'What job?'

'Yes.' Samantha crossed her fingers. 'Quite a good opportunity. You remember my telling you about that student of mine, Andrea Cole?'

'Not really.'

Samantha wasn't surprised. Ambrose had too many important things on his mind. 'Well, she's excellent,' she went on, undeterred by his lack of enthusiasm. 'Really top-notch. And I've had an offer to take her on as a private student this summer.'

'Just her?'

'Well, yes. Her family are quite wealthy. They want her to have the best available. And they seem to want her to have a chaperon of sorts, too. A companion, so to speak.'

'My dear, really, I can find you something... I don't think——'

'But I want to,' Samantha insisted. What she wanted was for her father not to feel sorry for her. She wanted just this once not to disappoint him.

She knew Ambrose too well, and if he thought she needed a job, he'd find her one. Only if he thought she had one would he go off to China confident that she was managing on her own.

'I could try to wangle you a visa, take you to China.'

'No, really——'

'You could come along, like old times...'

'I want to do this, Daddy.'

Ambrose sighed. 'I hope you know what you're doing.' Samantha knew he didn't think much of her teaching job. 'A lot of fiddle-faddle, do-re-mi and all that,' he'd dismissed it. Bothering with the instruction of 'the masses', as Ambrose called them, had never appealed to him. Samantha never disputed his view, but she didn't share it. In fact she genuinely liked teaching, even children who were never going to do more than play for their own enjoyment. But she knew even Ambrose would have found something to praise in Andrea Cole. It was too bad, in fact, that Samantha hadn't been telling him the truth.

'I'll be fine,' Samantha assured him.

'Well——'

'I promise.'

Three days later she was sitting in the middle of her living-room floor with the job ads spread out around her as she circled all the possible positions she might be qualified for—which weren't many—when the telephone rang.

'Hello?'

'Ms Peabody?' The voice was deep, drawling and decidedly masculine. It sent a shiver right up Samantha's spine.

'Yes?'

'Jason Cole here.'

Another shiver hit her, more devastating than the first. Why now, of all times? Samantha swallowed and took a deep breath. 'I already told you, Mr Cole——'

'You apparently told me a big fat lie, Ms Peabody,' he cut in.

'What?'

'I think, in fact, that it was a pretty juvenile way to handle things, and I'm not sure I approve, but since I still haven't hired anyone else and Andrea's still dead set on having you, I'm glad to hear you've accepted my offer.'

CHAPTER TWO

'I DON'T——'

'Why didn't you just say you had to get Daddy's approval first?'

'Daddy?' Oh, heavenly days!

'I trust we passed inspection?' The sarcasm fairly dripped from Jason's voice.

Samantha's chagrin vanished. She was suddenly seething. 'I don't know, Mr Cole. Did you? What did you talk about?'

'Mostly what a dear, sweet girl you were. And how lucky we were to get you.'

Oh, dear. 'Daddy said that?'

'Indeed he did. You could have taught Pablo Casals, the way he described it. Told me every single teacher you'd had since day one. Most notably, I understand, himself.'

'My father is a fantastic violinist.'

'So he said.' Jason's voice was as dry as the Sahara. 'In any case, since he seems amenable, I gather that you've changed your mind.'

'Well, I...' Samantha's eyes scanned the pages and pages of ads. They lit momentarily on the handful of jobs she was qualified for. In her mind she could see the millions of other girls who were doubtless equally qualified. The only thing she did well was teach the cello. Not one ad wanted her to do that.

Jason Cole did. But she didn't want to work for Jason Cole!

Still, she wouldn't be working for Jason Cole, her rational mind argued. Not really. He might be paying her, but she'd be working for his sister. She might not even see him. A high-powered businessman had little time to waste on his sister's teacher.

And again and again she'd thought how much she'd like to teach his sister. She'd made great progress with Andrea this year. Andrea was the most gifted fifteen-year-old cellist she'd ever seen, and certainly the best she'd ever had the privilege of teaching. It was a real temptation.

Besides, if she taught Andrea, she might possibly begin making a name for herself as a teacher—a person her father might also be proud of. But was it worth a summer of Jason Cole?

She sighed. She hemmed. She hawed.

'Maybe Andrea was wrong about you,' the voice on the other end of the line drawled softly. 'Maybe your father was wrong. Maybe you don't have the talent for it after all.'

Samantha straightened with a snap. 'I'll do it.'

There came a satisfied chuckle. 'Somehow, Ms Peabody, I thought you would.'

Andrea was thrilled. 'You're really coming?'

'Well, yes, I——'

'Fantastic!' Andrea pirouetted around Samantha's tiny kitchen, nearly knocking the teapot from the older girl's hands. 'When you said "no" at first, I was afraid you meant it. I almost gave up then. I'm glad I went ahead and convinced her.'

'Convinced who?'

'My Aunt Hortense.'

Samantha frowned as she poured out tea for both of them and handed Andrea a cup. 'Who is Aunt Hortense?'

'My great-aunt. She's my co-guardian. Along with Jason. She's very particular. Right out of the Dark Ages,

Jason says. He says she was born wearing a corset and an iron helmet.' Andrea giggled.

Samantha thought it sounded like the sort of thing a pushy businessman would say about an old lady with her niece's best interests at heart.

'After he met you, he said she'd never allow it anyway. You were too young and too beautiful.'

Jason Cole had said that? Oh, lord.

'But I convinced her,' Andrea went on.

'You did? How?'

'Oh, yes. I told her what a good teacher you were, what a good influence, what a——'

'Oh, please!'

'Well, it's true,' Andrea protested. 'I told her how mature you were, how responsible and dedicated . . . and she finally said OK. I guess she thought you might be too young,' Andrea added. 'She wouldn't have wanted us to go with Jason on tour if you were.'

Samantha frowned. 'On tour? What tour?'

'Just weekends. He only plays at weekends,' Andrea said quickly. 'That's when Aunt Hortense thinks I need someone to be with me.'

Samantha wasn't quite following. 'Plays?'

'Not every weekend either. And sometimes he plays in California.'

'Plays?' Samantha said again. 'I thought your family owned a sportswear company. I thought he was head of it.'

'He is. He has to be. It was Daddy's company, and Jason took it over when Daddy died. He didn't really want to. But he's done wonders with it, really. Everyone says so. Still, it isn't his main interest.'

Samantha was surprised to hear it. If anyone was born to pinstripes and power, it was Jason Cole. Still, it was something of a relief to discover that there was more to the man than balance sheets and profit margins. Her opinion improved slightly at the thought of his being good enough to go on tour at weekends. 'Does he play cello, too?'

'Er—no. Not cello.' Andrea contemplated her teacup, then looked up again and said brightly, 'Piano.'

Samantha, remembering his hands, felt a brief stab of satisfaction at her deduction. 'Really? Where's he playing this summer?'

'I'm not sure, actually,' Andrea said. 'Some places in California near our home, in Florida and Colorado. Wisconsin, too. And New York.'

'City?'

Andrea shook her head. 'Long Island, I think. You know, where Germaine's family has a summer place.'

Germaine was another of the strings students whom Samantha taught. 'The Hamptons?'

'Yes. That's it.'

Could Jason Cole be playing on the same programme as Oliver and her father? The thought intrigued Samantha, tantalised her. Of course, only playing at weekends, more for joy than for vocation, Jason wouldn't be the high-calibre musician that her father and Oliver were. But it was certainly more than she would've hoped. For all his Neanderthal tendencies, Jason Cole must have a bit of sensitivity after all.

And he was gorgeous. If Oliver showed up at the Hamptons concert with the buxom Nell Strickland in tow, Samantha thought she might actually enjoy meeting him in the company of Jason Cole. That would make Oliver sit up and take notice. Perhaps then he might stop waffling around, hinting about the future, and actually do something about it.

Perhaps, if it precipitated a proposal from Oliver, a summer spent in proximity to a man like Jason Cole might be worth enduring.

School ended the second week in June. Jason Cole had arranged for four non-stop airline tickets to Los Angeles the day after. Two for Andrea and Samantha. Two for their cellos. He had sent Samantha a contract in the same envelope.

It was all very straightforward. Wednesdays and every other Monday off, a generous salary, a room of her own at his home in Manhattan Beach, and transport provided when necessary to accompany the Coles. A firm twelve-week commitment between Samantha Aurelia Peabody and Jason Thomas Cole—no termination unless mutually agreed upon, and not a loophole in sight.

Samantha scrutinised the document again, lips pressed together in a firm line as she tried to figure out if she was about to sign her life away or not. Then she thought about the alternatives: tagging along after Oliver or her father, finding an even less appetising job. She sighed, then drew a deep breath and lifted her chin.

She could regard it as a test, she told herself. And, when she'd proved herself, she would be all that much worthier to call herself the daughter of Ambrose Peabody.

Samantha put her pen to the paper and signed it with a flourish. She kept one copy and posted the other back to Jason with a brief note. 'I am looking forward to working with Andrea,' she wrote. 'Perhaps the three of us can work on some trios.' She even made an effort to find some music for two cellos and piano to bring along with her.

Andrea looked doubtful and even a little uncomfortable when Samantha mentioned it, but Samantha didn't understand why.

At least, she didn't until the plane landed in Los Angeles that warm Wednesday evening.

She emerged from the tunnel, mentally girded to face the power-suited, tough-guy businessman who was to be her boss, and stared, horrified, as Andrea flew straight into the arms of a tall, muscular man with thick brown hair streaked with blond. A man wearing a pair of sand-coloured corduroy shorts and a bright blue T-shirt.

He was laughing, too, and hugging her back. Samantha, stunned, stopped dead right where she was until the woman behind her ploughed right into her and knocked her forward.

Jason disengaged himself from his sister and turned his gaze on her. It was an amused, knowing gaze, one that lifted the hairs on the back of Samantha's neck. His eyes raked her from the top of her head, taking in her freckles—practically counting them, Samantha thought irritably—her wide mouth, her almost boyish figure under her baggy blue peasant blouse and her full Paisley skirt, all the way down to the unpainted toenails that poked out the ends of her sandals.

'Ah, Ms Peabody, we meet again,' he drawled. 'And you're just as beautiful as ever.'

Samantha drew herself up to her full five feet nine inches, and for the first time found herself wishing for a few more. She hadn't remembered that he was quite so tall, but he towered a good five inches over her.

'Good evening, Mr Cole,' she said tightly, doing her best to ignore the unholy gleam in his eye.

Why wasn't he wearing a suit? She was prepared for dark pinstripes, white shirt, dark tie. She hadn't liked it, but she'd known how to deal with it.

She didn't know how to deal with him like this.

If he was daunting, arrogant and sexy in grey pin-stripes, in shorts and a T-shirt he was even worse. There was more tanned, hair-roughened flesh visible, for one thing. More blatant masculinity. More sheer animal magnetism. Samantha closed her eyes and thought of Oliver.

Then she opened them again and forced herself to focus on his hands. Piano-player's hands, she reminded herself. They were piano-player's hands.

But they seemed larger and more dangerous than ever as they gripped the handle of Andrea's cello case. They might, she conceded grudgingly, be piano-playing hands, but they looked as if they'd be more comfortable stroking the soft flesh of a woman—a thought she shoved ruthlessly aside—or wrapped around someone's throat. He'd be a man who'd play Beethoven, she thought. She said as much.

Jason looked at her as if she'd gone right round the bend. 'What in the hell are you talking about?' he demanded, picking up her cello, too.

'The music.'

'What music?'

'For your... your tour.'

Beside her she heard Andrea groan softly.

Jason stopped dead, his eyes going from Samantha to his sister. 'Music? For the tour? What in heaven's name have you been telling her?'

Andrea took a hasty step backward. 'Nothing really, Jason. I—she—well... I mentioned going with you on tour...and she...she asked——' Andrea swallowed hard '—she asked if you played cello, too.'

'And you said?'

'And, I said... well... I said no, but that you played piano. You do, you know,' she added defensively.

Jason simply stared at her.

Then, just when Samantha thought he'd turned to stone, his gaze swivelled and stormy blue eyes collided with her own. 'You've been had, Ms Peabody,' he said flatly.

'Had?' Samantha repeated, her voice a faint echo of his.

Jason nodded grimly. 'Had. I can play chopsticks on the piano. Barely. I play volleyball.'

He didn't play the piano. He played... volleyball?
Volleyball?

She sat down quite suddenly, grateful that the gods had placed a bench directly behind her before she'd dropped. Volleyball?

What little contact Samantha had had with volleyball had been hateful at best. All she could remember were the two years she hadn't travelled with her father, but had instead spent at a private school in upstate New York. There, on frosty spring mornings, she and a dozen other girls had been sent outside to bash fat white balls over impossibly high nets and had ended up with sprained fingers, skinned knees and stinging palms. As a sport, she ranked it somewhere below roller-skating.

'Beach volleyball,' Jason went on implacably. 'Professional beach volleyball.'

Samantha's mind spun. 'For money?' she asked, aghast, before she could stop herself.

'Yes,' he said flatly. 'For money. On tour. And this year my sportswear company is a major sponsor for five of the opens, so I've got administrative responsibilities as well.'

'You should see him play. He's good,' Andrea told her quickly. 'Very good.'

Samantha looked again at the tall, lithe, muscular body. He would be.

'You don't approve, Ms Peabody?' Jason lifted a sardonic brow.

Samantha opened her mouth but nothing came out. In her mind she saw herself arriving at the Hamptons with a volleyball player. She imagined Oliver's reaction. She imagined her father's.

'Well, don't let it worry you, sweetheart,' Jason said when she didn't reply. 'You just teach cello and keep Andrea on the straight and narrow, and you'll do just fine.'

Andrea blushed. 'Jason! I've never—I won't——'

'No, you won't.' Jason smiled and gave his sister's long blonde braid a tug. 'But there are plenty of guys who'll want to, believe me.'

Samantha felt a twinge of worry. It became far more than a twinge when he went on, 'And they'll take one look at Ms Priss here——' he nodded at Samantha '—and they'll want her, too.'

She felt the hunger of his gaze as it roved over her and she began to burn.

Then he smiled mockingly at her. 'Or they will until she looks down her nose like that and turns 'em to stone. Hortense wanted someone who was fifty and wore sensible shoes. I was surprised when Andi said she agreed to you, but now I see why. You'll probably do just fine. Let's go.' And he started down the corridor, Andrea at his side.

Samantha didn't move. She was rooted to the spot. All her instincts told her to stay right where she was or—even better—to jump back on the plane and head back to JFK.

She'd been out of her mind, taking this job. She was out of her depth. In far over her head. It was not the sort of thing she should have done at all. Of course she could handle the teaching part. She'd never worried about that. She'd even thought she could manage the chaperoning. After all, she knew Andrea, and she knew artists, musicians, men of talent and sensitivity—all the men inhabiting the world Andrea would most likely be moving in. She could deal with them.

She thought she could even have managed in a world populated by steely-eyed businessmen. At least she'd been schooled in how to defend herself against them. Her father had seen to that. Another Louis Lambert or Fritz Hoffmann—even one as heart-stoppingly handsome and charming as Andrea's brother—she would have coped with.

But volleyball players? *Beach bums?* Oh, help!

Halfway down the corridor, Jason stopped. He turned suddenly and looked at her. 'Having second thoughts, sweetheart? Didn't scare you, did I?'

'Jason!' Andrea admonished.

He smiled. 'Don't worry,' he said with the barest hint of kind condescension. 'No one's going to jump your bones. Least of all me,' he added. 'I like my women willing, Ms Peabody. And there are plenty who are.'

Jason led them to the baggage claim area, then out into the warmth of the Southern California evening. Samantha and Andrea, each with a suitcase, trailed after him as he led them past rows of vehicles.

Samantha wasn't wholly surprised—only horrified—when he stopped beside an open-topped Jeep Renegade.

Jason took one look at her and grinned, saying to Andrea, 'Maybe she is fifty, after all. Or a hundred and fifty, come to that.'

'Jason!' Andrea admonished again. 'He doesn't mean it,' she told Samantha.

Samantha doubted that. She thought Jason meant every word, and, what was more, was enjoying saying them. He knew straight away that he could get a rise out of her and was determined to do so. Irritated, she flung her suitcase into the back alongside Andrea's and brushed past him to climb in, stepping down hard on his instep in the process.

Jason's eyebrows lifted. 'Sweet little thing, aren't you?' he said through clenched teeth. 'For a Daddy's girl.'

Samantha stared straight ahead and held on tight.

A good thing, too, for Jason seemed intent on giving her the ride of her life. He whipped the Jeep in and out of the traffic, zipping out of the airport maze with the ease of a New York cab driver, then heading straight west.

'We'll take the ocean road,' he hollered over the roar of the traffic. 'Prettier that way.' He flashed her a wide grin and gave her a blatant wink. 'You'll love it.'

No, she wouldn't.

But unfortunately it was difficult not to. The sun was setting over the Pacific, casting the entire scene in a seductive golden orange glow. Used to the grit, grime and bustle of New York, Samantha was amazed at the wide, almost deserted white sand beach stretching along the right side of the road. She felt as if it were a postcard, not a reality. And she wasn't sure she was glad it was not.

It, like Jason Cole, seemed far too powerful and seductive. The whole ambience had an aura of make-believe, like Oz. She felt as if, were she to screw her eyes shut tight and then—quick as a flash—open them again, like Dorothy and Toto, she would be back in Kansas. She tried; unfortunately it didn't work.

'We'll be home just in time for a dip in the surf!' Jason shouted over the roar of a jet. 'You like to swim?'

Swim? Samantha shuddered. That was the last thing she wanted, but she wasn't saying so. If Jason Cole knew the way she felt about water, he'd probably throw her in just for the heck of it.

She managed a tight smile, clenched the side of the Jeep and tried to pretend that her knuckles were always that shade of white.

'Home sweet home,' Jason announced fifteen minutes later as he pulled into the garage behind a beachfront house and bounded out of the Jeep, wrestling both cello cases out after him.

Andrea grabbed her suitcase and followed him eagerly. Samantha took her time. She felt as if every step she took might set off a mine.

Jason's house was a low and sprawling, redwood and glass contemporary set right across a broad pavement from the white sand beach. He led them up the front steps to a wide porch scattered with deckchairs, set the cellos down and unlocked the door.

The living-room was tastefully and casually furnished with a broad stone fireplace, soft leather furniture, a beige-coloured Berber-style carpet, a sophisticated telephone and answering machine apparatus and what looked like a state-of-the-art weight bench. The quintessential bachelor pad. None of it surprised Samantha in the least.

What did surprise her was that, even in spite of those things, the house looked lived-in and almost homey. There were framed pictures of the family on the mantel, and newspapers, magazines and books scattered about. Several pairs of jeans and a stack of freshly laundered T-shirts were folded on the dining-room table, obviously waiting for Jason to put them away. A game of solitaire, half-played, lay on the coffee-table.

Solitaire? An odd notion—Jason Cole alone. It made him seem human, somehow, even vulnerable. How unnerving. Samantha looked away.

Jason pointed Andrea towards her room, then took Samantha into the one next door, deposited her cello in the corner and opened the wardrobe so she could see all the space available to her.

'All yours,' he said. 'You can just set your suitcase in there for now and have a look at the rest of the place in the morning. Suit you?'

'It's fine,' she said.

'Ah, a hint of amenability at last.'

Samantha scowled.

Jason grinned and winked at her, then headed back towards the hallway. 'Don't bother putting things away. Just get a suit on now and come on.'

'Suit?'

'Swimsuit.'

'Oh.' She shook her head and knotted her fingers together in front of her. 'No, thank you.'

Jason stopped in the doorway and turned, looking at her blankly. 'Why not? What's wrong now?'

'Nothing. I just don't want a swim.'

He stared at her. 'You aren't serious?'

'I'm perfectly serious. I'm tired. It's been a hard day. I'll just take a shower and go right to bed.'

His brows drew together. He didn't move. One hand high against the door-jamb supported his weight as he frowned at her. 'You've been on a plane for hours.'

'I know that.'

He waved an arm towards the wide sandy beach on his doorstep. 'This is California, for heaven's sake, land of the lotus eaters. You spent the entire school year in grubby old high-pressure New York, and now you don't even want to enjoy the beach?'

'I am enjoying it,' Samantha said testily. 'From here.'

'It's not the same. Not the same at all.'

'Perhaps not to you.' Samantha sighed and raked a hand through her flyaway brown hair. Why couldn't he just leave her alone? Why this on top of everything else?

Jason was shaking his head as if he couldn't imagine her refusal. Then suddenly he stopped. 'I get it,' he said, a grin lifting the corner of his mouth.

'Get what?'

'What you're afraid of.'

Samantha looked at him, terrified that he had somehow discerned her deepest fear.

Then he winked at her. 'It's the iceberg syndrome. You're afraid if you go in the water you'll melt.'

Samantha shut the door in his face.

She took a shower, she brushed out her long, tangled hair. She put on a summer-weight nightgown, stretched out on the bed, and found herself staring at the ceiling. She couldn't sleep. She couldn't even close her eyes. If she did, she saw Jason Cole smirking at her on the undersides of her lids. She'd never in her life had to deal with a man like him.

Samantha clenched her fists against her sides and concentrated on breathing slowly and deeply. She tried thinking about where her father would be right now, where Oliver would be, what time it would be in Nanking, what time it would be in Hilton Head.

None of it did any good. It didn't matter. Nothing mattered but this—that she was here, and that she would be here for the next twelve weeks, and that somehow she was going to have to learn to cope with Jason Cole.

She'd hoped, of course, that her initial reaction to him—that intense physical awareness, that heightened sensitivity, which she'd experienced that afternoon in New York—had been an aberration.

It didn't appear to be. It was, if anything, worse. Jason Cole in a suit had been pigeonholeable. In a suit he'd been a man just like Fritz or Louis Lambert. A man unconcerned with anything other than his own needs and desires. A tough, powerful, determined man whom Samantha was equally determined to resist.

A Jason Cole in shorts and a T-shirt, grinning and hugging his sister, was something else.

No, she told herself sharply, he wasn't. He was still the same man with yet another guise. He was, in fact, quite possibly worse. He was a volleyball player, of all things. A jock. But he was also damnably attractive. And he knew it.

Not only to her, she was certain. She had no trouble imagining Jason attracting women. They probably fell at his feet when he walked by. Did volleyball players have groupies? No doubt she would find out. And, if they did, she was willing to bet Jason Cole would have more than his share.

She would have to be careful to maintain a strictly professional attitude around him. And she wasn't foolish enough to believe it would be easy. Jason Cole was a tease. He knew he unnerved her, and he revelled in it. But if she could hold herself aloof, ignore him—ignore the things just the sight of him did to her—then she would be safe.

Just then she heard the sound of voices outside on the porch. Andrea was saying something to her brother as they came back in from the beach. Samantha heard her soft voice, then her infectious giggle. Then Jason laughed, too. His laugh was low and appreciative, warm and masculine. The sort of laugh a man ought to have. The sort of laugh that sent a pleasurable shiver right down her spine.

Samantha groaned and pulled the pillow over her head.

Aloof. Aloof. Aloof.

There was a certain efficacy to the repetition of a mantra, according to her father. It focused the mind, honed the intellect, refined the sensibilities.

And Samantha just hoped that repeating it over and over again would help to remind her to begin her summer here as she meant to go on. That was another bit of Ambrose's sage advice, and she'd never felt its appropriateness more than now.

She began saying the word the moment she awoke. Though she hadn't slept particularly well, she found herself awake at shortly past seven and was restless the moment she opened her eyes.

The sound of movements beyond the closed door of her bedroom made her wonder if perhaps Andrea was already up before her. If so they could make an early start of it. She'd like to be in full swing by the time Andrea's brother appeared on the scene. Samantha scrambled out of bed and opened the blinds, taking a deep breath of salt-scented air and determining to make the best of things. Aloof, she said to herself. Whatever happened, she would be aloof.

She opened the door and found herself staring into Jason Cole's bare chest. Samantha took a quick step backward and fastened her gaze on her toes. But not soon enough. Not before she'd caught a very good glimpse of a tanned, hair-roughened chest and a hard, flat, equally sandy belly.

'You're up bright and early.' Jason gave her a wolfish smile as he paused in the hallway, the daunting chest just inches from her, a towel wrapped around his hips.

'Good morning,' she said to the floor.

'Sleep well?'

'Yes.' Still to the floor.

'Good.' He waited for a moment as if it was her turn to speak, but when she didn't he went on, 'Nice morning, isn't it?'

'Yes.'

'Not too hot.'

'No.' She wanted to get past him but there was no way she could do so without literally brushing him aside, a task she wouldn't have minded if it hadn't meant touching him.

He didn't move, just laughed at her now. 'Talkative, aren't you?'

Samantha felt her cheeks flame. Her father had always told her to ignore people like Jason Cole, and she was trying, lord knew. It just didn't seem to be going to work. She stood there, steeling herself for his next teasing remark.

It was a surprise, then, when Jason only said, almost kindly, 'I just finished practice and had a shower. You take yours and I'll rustle us up some breakfast.'

Before she could object he slipped past her. Astonished, heart still fluttering, Samantha turned and watched him go, her eyes fastened on the breadth of his tanned and muscular back.

Until she was standing under the icy-cold spray of the shower, the word 'aloof' never even entered her mind.

CHAPTER THREE

JASON was gone when she got out of the shower. In fact, he was gone for the rest of the day. But breakfast was waiting for her in the kitchen in the form of a bowl of sliced fresh strawberries, cold cereal and milk, and a freshly brewed pot of coffee.

Hesitantly, reluctantly, Samantha proceeded to eat. She certainly hadn't expected Jason Cole to make breakfast for her. She felt faintly uncomfortable that he had.

But, she thought, maybe he was trying to make up for all his earlier teasing comments. Maybe he had decided she was not the sort of woman he wanted to bother with. She could hope.

She made up her mind to spend the day setting the tone for the rest of the summer. Until lunch, she and Andrea worked over new material, then spent some time on old. Afterwards, at Andrea's insistence, they went to the beach. Andrea swam and Samantha sat on a beach towel, watching, still wearing her full skirt and scoop-necked blouse, a fact that had Andrea in fits.

'You could at least put on a suit,' she exclaimed.

'I don't have one.'

'We can go shopping.'

'No.' It seemed far wiser, if one didn't want to end up in the water, not to imply by one's mode of dress that there was any possibility that one did.

'What about a pair of shorts and a shirt, then?' Andrea said. 'Wouldn't you be more comfortable?'

'I'm fine,' Samantha said. Though it was less comfortable than she'd thought to spend the afternoon tucking her skirt around her legs lest the wind whip it up.

She was glad when, after four and a half hours, at last Andrea had had enough and they trekked back up the beach to the house.

Jason was just coming out. He wore only a pair of shorts and had a towel slung around his neck. He grinned as they clambered up the sand, then held out a hand to hoist first Andrea, then Samantha over the wall on to the broad pavement called the Strand.

Samantha declined. 'I can manage.'

Jason frowned, then shrugged. 'Suit yourself.' He dropped nimbly over the wall and landed with a soft thud on the sand beside her.

Samantha ignored his closeness, turning instead to try the wall again. But it was higher than she'd thought, and the wind was lifting her skirt as she did so. She clutched at it futilely, then made a sound of strangled annoyance, shoved the skirt between her knees, anchoring it, and pressed both palms on the wall to push.

Suddenly there was a firm pressure against her bottom and she felt herself being lifted on to the wall. Just as suddenly the pressure was gone. She whipped around to glower at Jason.

He smiled. 'Don't thank me.' And sketching her a quick salute, he turned on his heel. 'You'd better put something on that face of yours, Ms Peabody, my dear,' he said over his shoulder. 'You've got one heck of a sunburn.'

So she did. She felt, as the day went on, as if the sun had taken up residence inside her. The parts of her that had been covered by her skirt and blouse had been somewhat protected, though her gauzy blouse had let through more of the sun's rays than she would have liked. But her face, her neck and just below it, her forearms, her calves and the tops of her feet were a brilliant red.

'Didn't you use sun-screen?' Jason demanded when he came back from the beach volleyball courts two hours later and found Samantha sitting in the living-room radiating heat.

'I didn't think it would be necessary,' she said stiffly. 'I was dressed.'

'Doesn't make any difference. Why didn't you tell her?' He glowered at Andrea, who was about to go out for pizza with two girls she'd met swimming that afternoon.

'Don't blame Andrea,' Samantha said firmly. 'It was my own stupid fault. Go on,' she said to the younger girl. 'Have a good time.'

'You're sure you don't want to come?'

Samantha shook her head. 'No, thanks.' She managed a grim smile. 'I'll just sit here and read a book.' And glow, she thought privately as the girls vanished out of the door.

'Do you have a fever?' Jason reached out and laid his palm against her forehead before she could move away.

'No!' She slipped quickly away from him.

'Well, you should have some ointment on it,' Jason decreed.

'I don't have any.'

He frowned, then turned on his heel and headed for the bathroom. She could hear him muttering and rummaging about. A few minutes later he reappeared. 'I'll run uptown and get some at the drug store.'

'It's not necessary,' Samantha said quickly.

Jason snorted. 'Want to bet?'

Before she could say another word, he'd pulled on a shirt and was out of the door.

Samantha considered locking herself in her room before he got back, but rejected it for the immature notion that it was. Still, he made her feel like an idiot. She was an idiot. And she was an even bigger idiot fussing about it; he was just doing what any thoughtful employer would do. But all the same she didn't want to be beholden to him.

Especially not when he reappeared twenty minutes later, looked down at her and said, 'Strip.'

Samantha goggled at him. 'I beg your pardon?'

'I'll rub it on you. But I can't do it when you're all covered up.'

'I'm not any more covered now than I was on the beach.'

'You really wore that idiotic outfit to the beach?'

'You saw what I was wearing.'

'That's ridiculous.'

'That's your opinion.' Samantha lifted her chin and looked up at him stubbornly. 'But I do thank you for the ointment——' she held out her hand '—which, if you will just give me, I will put on.'

'Let me see.'

'What?'

'Show me your burn.'

'You can see my burn.' She glared at him. 'Look at my face!'

'Show me where it ends, I mean.'

If it had been possible to blush any redder than she already was, Samantha would have done so then. 'You mean...pull down the neck of my top?'

Jason gave her a leering smirk. 'That'd be nice. Or you could lift your skirt.'

Samantha could almost feel the steam coming out of her ears. 'I don't think so.'

'I told you I don't jump unwilling women. Don't be a prude.'

'I'm not a prude!'

'What would you call it?'

She got hastily to her feet. 'I call it being sensible. If you won't just give it to me, fine. I'll go buy my own.' She started towards the door, but Jason caught her by the arm.

'Don't be an idiot, Samantha. Of course I'll give it to you.' But he didn't. Not immediately. They stood facing each other, his hand still on her arm, her eyes fastened on his grip, her mind focused on the gentle strength with which he held her. It felt warm and possessive. No, not really possessive—concerned.

Yeah, sure, Samantha thought. It was all too clear what Jason Cole really wanted.

He let go of her arm at last and lifted a hand to touch the tip of her nose with his index finger. Then he gave her a rueful smile and laid the tube of ointment in her palm. 'Why are you afraid of me, Samantha?'

'I'm not afraid of you!'

'So what's the problem, then?'

She shifted uncomfortably under his gaze. 'I'm not used to being teased,' she said finally.

'No brothers?'

She shook her head.

'Sisters?'

Another negative shake.

'I should have guessed.'

She slanted him a glance. 'Why?'

'Daddy is a bit over-protective.'

Samantha stiffened. 'He's a wonderful father.'

Jason took a step backwards and stood against the door-jamb, holding up his palms as if to ward off an attack. 'Hey, OK. I never said he wasn't. I just should have guessed you were his only one. You must be very close, your family.'

'I'm very close to my father.'

'What about your mother?'

'No.'

'Is she dead?'

'They're . . . divorced.'

Jason's brows hiked up into the fringe of his sun-bleached hair. 'And Daddy got custody?'

'She left us,' Samantha said bitterly before she could stop herself.

'Ah.'

'We got along just fine without her,' Samantha said abruptly. She didn't know why she was telling him this. It wasn't something she talked about. And it was certainly none of his business.

Jason shifted his weight against the door-jamb. 'Mmm.' He was looking at her seriously now. There was no sign of the teasing glint she often saw lurking in his gaze. He pressed his lips together in a thin line, then nodded slightly. What was he thinking? Was he feeling sorry for her? Samantha bristled.

'Go put this on,' he told her after a moment, indicating the ointment. 'I'll get a shower and we'll go out for dinner.'

'No, thank you.'

Jason gave her a level look. 'What?'

'You don't need to buy me dinner.'

'I know I don't *need* to buy you dinner. I want to.'

'No, thank you.'

'Do you work for me?' The question was so soft she almost didn't hear it.

'Work for you?'

'That's what I said.'

'Of course.'

'Then we'll have dinner.'

There was no room for argument with his tone. It was calm, matter-of-fact. Samantha drew a deep breath, tried to think of some way around his implacability. But just at that moment her stomach growled.

Jason grinned.

Samantha sped down the hall to the safety of her room.

She went to dinner with him. She had no choice. The restaurant Jason chose was a quiet, California-style, low-slung building, not overly posh. Its menu relied heavily on broiled fresh-caught fish, zesty Mexican dishes, and lots of fresh vegetables. He led her wordlessly down several steps into the cosy adobe-walled dining-room where the *maître d'* greeted him by name.

'So nice to see you again, Mr Cole. We have an excellent table just for you.'

They were led to a table hidden away behind a huge Boston fern, where Jason held Samantha's chair for her before he sat down across from her.

Her amazement must have been obvious, because he grinned. 'You expected maybe a burrito?'

Samantha looked down, embarrassed at her transparency. 'I didn't expect anything.'

'No, you probably didn't,' Jason said after a moment. 'But I think it's time you realised I have a few manners up my sleeve after all.'

'You even have sleeves tonight,' Samantha replied tartly.

Jason grinned. *'Touché.'*

Immediately she looked away. No matter how she tried, she couldn't seem to master immunity to that grin. Even now it could dampen her palms and make her heart thrum in her chest. Deliberately she stared at the woven, richly coloured place-mat and tried to muster her defences.

'Would you like a drink?' Jason asked.

Samantha shook her head. Alcohol was the last thing she needed tonight. 'No, thank you. But you go right ahead.' She flicked her lashes up long enough to see him give a negative shake of his head at the waiter.

The waiter handed her an oversized menu. She ducked behind it, perusing it mindlessly, trying to regain her equilibrium, not bothering to read it at all, knowing the ordering would be taken care of.

When the waiter returned, Jason looked at her expectantly. 'Have you decided what you'd like?'

Flustered, Samantha stared at him. Her father had always ordered for her. So had Oliver.

'You—I——'

'I don't know what you'd like,' he said simply.

She scanned the menu quickly. 'I'll have the swordfish and a salad.'

'Sounds good. I'll have the same.' Then he chose a wine to complement her choice. 'Suit you? Or would you prefer one not so dry?'

'No. No, it's fine.'

The waiter took the menus from them and nodded smartly. 'I'll be right back with your salads.'

His sudden absence made Samantha more aware than ever of the man across the table from her. She felt awkward and nervous, the way she used to feel at a recital right before she had to play. But, just as a difficult piece was easier if tackled straight on, so would dealing with Jason be if she got the conversation off on the right track.

She picked up her water glass and took a sip, then straightened her spine, lifted her chin and met his gaze. 'I suppose you'd like to talk about Andrea.'

'I'd rather talk about you...'

Samantha choked.

Jason rose and half leaned across the table. 'Are you all right?'

Her cheeks flamed, and not from the sunburn! 'I don't want——' she spluttered the moment she could speak.

'But since you seem to get prickly whenever the subject comes up,' Jason went on blandly, as if she hadn't even spoken, 'we'll start out talking about Andrea.' He sat back down and gave her a disarming smile. 'I hadn't heard her play much before I went out to New York this spring. I was astonished. She's very good.'

Samantha swallowed and took a deep breath. 'Yes, she's excellent.' She grasped this new topic with both hands, though she didn't think for one minute she was entirely safe. Jason was too clever. 'For one so young, she's quite remarkable.'

'Good teaching,' Jason said easily. He took the wine that the waiter offered, tasted it, nodded, then handed Samantha the glass.

Samantha hesitated but, when he still held it out to her, she tasted it too, and, when she saw that he was waiting for it, nodded her approval. Her cheeks felt warm again. Due to the wine this time, she hoped, and not the way his blue eyes seemed suddenly almost to be caressing her.

'I wish good teaching were all it took,' she said, determined to keep them on the topic of his sister. 'But Andrea is the only student of such outstanding quality that it's been my privilege to teach.'

He poured the wine and passed her a glass. 'Have you taught long?'

She sipped it gratefully. It was light and dry, and she found that it made talking easier. 'Just a year.'

'Do you like it?'

'Yes. Enormously. Much more than I expected,' she admitted. She took another swallow of the wine, liking it very much.

Jason leaned back against his chair, smiling slightly, listening intently, his eyes warm. 'Why didn't you expect to?'

Samantha shrugged, feeling a bit self-conscious. 'It wasn't what I'd planned.'

'What had you planned?'

'To be the next Pablo Casals.' Samantha grimaced slightly. 'Or Rostropovich.'

He ran an idle finger around the rim of his wine glass. 'Lofty goals.'

'Performance is all,' Samantha said solemnly.

'What?'

'Performance is all. That's what my father says.'

'Good old Daddy.'

'I don't know why you talk about him in that tone of voice.'

Jason shrugged. 'Gut instinct, maybe. Never mind. So he's a good violinist, is he?'

'Good? He's one of the very best, most talented——'

'Yeah, I get the picture. And he thinks you ought to be, too?' Jason was regarding her solemnly over the top of his wine glass.

'He did.'

'Did?'

'I'm not good enough.'

Jason frowned. 'Is that what he said?'

'Oh, my, no. He'd never say anything. He doesn't have to. I can tell. I can see the way he looks at me sometimes when he doesn't think I see him.'

'Oh? How's that?'

Samantha sighed and took a sip of her wine. 'Sort of sad. You know. Like he's tried his best, but it just won't work. And he's right.'

'What about you?'

The question was soft. Samantha wasn't even sure she'd heard it right. 'What?'

'I said, what about you? Is that what you wanted, too?' Jason's eyes bored into hers.

'Well, I—of course, I did,' Samantha said irritably.

He smiled. 'Of course. What do you want now?'

'Now?'

'Now that you're not going to be Pablo.'

'I . . . I'm going to get married.'

'Is that all?'

'All?' Samantha stared at him to see if he was teasing, but he appeared perfectly serious.

His broad shoulders lifted. 'I thought you liked teaching.'

'Well, I do, but . . .'

'So can't you be married and teach?'

'No.'

'No?' Jason frowned.

Samantha met his gaze firmly. 'No.'

The waiter brought their salads then, thank heavens. Samantha didn't want to get into an argument with Jason, but the way he was looking she was sure that she would. He would never understand the sort of care and nurturing that a man like Ambrose or Oliver required. There would be no time for her to teach.

And anyway, she suddenly realised that, though she'd declined to talk about herself at the start of the conversation, he had led her right into that very topic! Jason Cole was a very wily opponent.

She took another swallow of her wine and concentrated on the salad. Cold asparagus tips on a bed of lettuce with a subtly mustard-flavoured house dressing whose herbs she could only guess, it was delicate and tasty.

'Beats burritos, doesn't it?' Jason grinned at her.

Samantha nodded. 'I've never had one.'

'I'm sure we can rectify that.'

'It really isn't necessary,' she said quickly, not wanting to spend any more time with him than she had to.

'I think it is.'

'But——'

'You don't have to try one if you don't want to,' Jason said equably. 'But I know a great Mexican place in Hermosa. We can go there next week.'

'But——'

'Don't tell me it's beneath you.'

Samantha bristled. 'Why on earth would you think that?'

'Maybe because you walk around like the rest of us *peons* are going to give you a disease.'

'I never!'

'No?'

There was a wealth of scepticism in that one word. Samantha was about to take exception to it, but the waiter arrived again, bearing off the salad plates and setting out their main course.

Jason dug in as if he were starving, so the conversation came to an end. Samantha was hungry, too, and when she was eating she didn't have to keep defending herself. She bent her head and gave the plate her full attention. She didn't like the idea that Jason felt she was a snob. But if it kept him at a distance, perhaps it wasn't such a bad thing.

When she had finished, she considered the danger of letting Jason pick the next avenue of conversation and decided to try one herself. 'You should really be beginning to prepare Andrea for her university career.'

'I am.'

'Oh?'

'I've hired you. You're the best thing that's happened to Andrea.'

Samantha ducked her head. 'I don't think——'

'Stop being so damned modest. Who knocked off your self-esteem?'

Her head jerked up. 'I beg your pardon?'

He grinned at her unrepentantly. 'Ah, good. You do have a little. It just seems to get covered over about nine-tenths of the time.'

'Really, Mr Cole——'

'Jason.'

'You're my employer.'

'So you'll call me what I tell you. What gives with you, Samantha Peabody?' He was looking at her with curiosity.

Samantha ground her teeth. 'I don't have to explain myself to you.'

'No, I guess not. But then——' he grinned '—you'll just have to put up with me poking around till I find out.'

'You have no call to "poke around" in my life at all.'

'Of course I do.'

She stared at him. 'Why?'

'I'm your employer,' he shot back.

She glared.

He grinned. 'Because I'm interested in you.'

'Well, I'm not interested in you!'

'No?'

'No! I'm already interested in someone else! I told you that!'

'Ah, yes. The flautist.' He said the word with the same enthusiasm that Ambrose would say 'volleyball player'.

'Oliver is a wonderful, talented, sensitive musician.'

Jason laughed. 'Oh, great. I can just imagine the kids you two will have.'

'Kids? We're not having any kids!'

'No,' he said. 'I don't suppose you would. He probably doesn't even know how. Him being such a rarefied type and all.'

Samantha wished she dared throw her water glass at him. 'You don't know the first thing about Oliver. He's got higher things on his mind. Just because all you think about is sex!'

'What's wrong with sex?'

Samantha felt her cheeks burn. 'You Neanderthal types are all alike!'

Jason's grin broadened. Then he leaned across the table and stole a smacking kiss. 'Is that a compliment?'

'You know very well it's not!'

'Didn't think so.' He winked. 'But whether I'm Neanderthal or not, you're right about one thing, sweetheart. You do make me think about sex.'

Samantha's fork clattered to the plate.

'And you think about it, too, my lovely. And you know it.'

'I never——'

'Bull,' he said bluntly. 'Be glad. It's better than being all repressed. Healthier.' He gave her a smug grin.

Samantha shoved her plate away. 'I'd like to leave now.'

'Getting you hot and bothered?'

'Yes! I mean, no! Damn you, Jason Cole!'

Jason's eyes grew wide as he feigned shock. 'The lady can swear.' His blue eyes glinted.

The lady could do a damned sight more than that, Samantha thought. 'I want to leave,' she said through clenched teeth.

Jason didn't move. 'Not polite,' he chided her. 'Never force your host to leave before he's had his cup of after-dinner coffee. Didn't your father teach you anything?'

'My father taught me never to deal with men like you.'

Jason shook his head. 'It figures.'

Samantha glowered at him, steaming at his sarcasm, wanting to leave, yet unsure how to force him to comply.

'Calm down,' Jason said to her. 'Sit back, finish your meal, enjoy your cup of coffee and relax.'

Samantha gave him a wary, distrustful look. Relax? How? The moment she did, he lunged.

But as if he'd abruptly decided that lunging was no longer his style, Jason desisted. When the waiter had cleared away their plates and Samantha was on the edge of her chair, prepared to leave, instead she found him ordering a glass of cognac for himself and one for her. Then he encouraged the waiter to fill their coffee-cups again.

'I want——'

'I want you to hush.' He gave her a sweet smile. 'Come on, Samantha, sparring time's over.'

She gave him a distrustful look.

He patted her hand. 'Did Andrea ever tell you about the time she was being taught by Aunt Hortense?'

Samantha shook her head.

Jason grinned and proceeded to relate a marvellously funny anecdote about the determination of his battleaxe aunt faced with the overwhelming talent of his little sister. Then he went on to recount several more stories about Andrea's childhood which were designed to disarm Samantha and to enchant her as well.

He was, to Samantha's chagrin, quite successful. Jason Cole was a good storyteller, full of wit and charm. Samantha already knew that, of course. She'd seen glimpses of it often enough before tonight. But even knowing that, she couldn't help falling for it.

It was so pleasant. So suddenly unthreatening. So nice to stop defending herself for the moment and just sit back and sip her cognac and listen to stories about the serious, intense little girl who had grown into Samantha's finest student. She liked the fact that Jason's pride in his sister was evident, too.

'You've taught her tons,' he said finally, regarding her solemnly over the top of his glass.

Samantha shook her head. 'Not really. I——'

'Stop it. You have. False modesty doesn't become you, Samantha. You're terrifically good with her. I can hear the progress she's made.' He shook his head in wonderment. 'Sometimes I don't know how you do it.'

Samantha inclined her head, grateful for the praise since this time it seemed genuine. 'I do what I can.'

In the background she heard the softly murmured conversations of the other diners, the subdued clink of silver against china, the soft sounds of Antonio Carlos Jobim from a speaker near the bar. She lifted her gaze to Jason's face and found his eyes fastened on her own. His expression was serious, but not daunting. His eyes, though grave, were warm as they met her own.

She felt a *frisson* of awareness prickle down her spine and lift the hairs on the back of her neck. And she discovered that her gaze, once captured, wouldn't move away.

One corner of Jason's mouth lifted. His hand reached out and, for a mere instant, brushed along her cheek, touching the single strand of hair that escaped her chignon. 'You are beautiful.' His words were hushed and a little hoarse.

Samantha's coffee-cup clattered noisily against the saucer as she tried to pick it up. 'No,' she contradicted. 'I'm not.' But her voice cracked as she spoke, mortifying her.

She gave up trying to drink and set the cup down firmly, then knotted her hands in her lap. Lifting her eyes, she met his gaze. 'Do you suppose we could please go now?' Her voice was a little wavery and plaintive, and she felt foolish, but even as she spoke she was already getting up. She couldn't remain any longer. Simply couldn't. It reminded her all too much of Fritz and his lies.

Jason sighed and tossed his napkin on to the table. 'By all means,' he said drily and followed her.

Why had he spoiled it? Samantha wondered as she stood, shifting from one foot to the other, waiting for him to pay the bill. Just when they were getting along at least reasonably well, why did he have to look at her that way, tell her she was beautiful?

It wasn't as if he were really attracted to her, even though he'd said he was. She wasn't the least bit Jason's type.

She had seen Jason's type. They were legion all over the beach. She'd seen them following him today. Legions of tall, leggy blondes, with gorgeous honey tans that didn't even end where their bathing-suits did, lavished all the attention on him any mortal man could wish for. And Jason ate it up, she'd seen him this afternoon giving them a grin, a teasing comment, a quick kiss.

And she knew from Andrea's conversation that one woman in particular—a model named Dena—occupied the bulk of his free time.

'They have an understanding,' Andrea had told her while they were still in New York and Samantha had ventured a question about Jason's marital status. Just what that understanding was, no one said. But if he dated women like Dena-the-model, there was no way he could consider Samantha beautiful. He was only having her on, making a play for her, trying to 'score' just for the sheer fun of it, like Fritz. And she'd been sucker enough to fall for it.

You fool, Samantha chastised herself, and, while Jason paid the bill, she stalked out of the restaurant as if he weren't even with her.

She didn't want to talk to him. She didn't even want to see him. She was furious—mostly with herself. She'd almost let him turn her head, just the way Fritz had, and the way her mother had let Louis Lambert turn hers. Samantha got in the Jeep, folded her hands in her lap and stared straight ahead. As far as she was concerned, they couldn't get home fast enough.

But when he got back in the Jeep beside her, Jason made no move to turn on the engine. He simply sat there and stared at her.

Samantha plucked at her skirt. 'Why aren't we going?'

'Because I want to know what got your back up in there.'

Samantha looked away. The cars zipping by down Pacific Coast Highway were an endless source of fascination.

Jason didn't move. 'I mean it, Sam. What gives?'

'My name's not Sam!'

'Samantha,' he corrected quietly. 'So, what's wrong? What happened? What did I say?'

Was he trying to pretend he didn't know? She pressed her lips together and knotted her fingers.

Still Jason waited.

Samantha thought she could wait longer. She was wrong. The traffic throbbed past. Far out over the Pacific a jet banked and curved southward. Minutes later another behind it began the same move. It became obvious that until he got an answer Jason Cole really wasn't going anywhere.

'It isn't true,' she muttered at last.

'What isn't?'

'We were talking perfectly normally and then, right out of the blue, you said I was beautiful!' She lifted her eyes and glared accusingly at him.

He looked at her in frank astonishment. 'You are.'

'I am not!'

'That's what made you mad?'

'Of course it made me mad. I don't like being patronised.' She wasn't going to come right out and accuse him of coming on to her.

'You think I was patronising you?' He sounded incredulous.

'Certainly. There are far more beautiful women than I am. Dozens. You see them every day.'

'Oh.' A pause. 'Of course.'

She gave him a baleful stare, which he returned with bland innocence. 'You do,' she insisted.

'All right.' He sounded weary now. 'Would it make you feel better if I told you that you weren't lovely in the least?'

'Yes.' Samantha was adamant.

'Fine. You're ugly as sin.' Jason flicked on the key, the engine roared to life, and the Jeep shot out of the car park. 'Happy now?' he shouted at her over the noise of the traffic.

Perversely, having got what she wanted, Samantha discovered that she didn't know if she was happy or not.

CHAPTER FOUR

JASON asked Samantha to take him to the airport in the morning.

'Aren't we coming, too?' Andrea wanted to know.

'Not this weekend.' Jason tossed a duffel bag on to the table and began packing it. 'I didn't know for sure when you were coming in from New York, so I didn't book any tickets. You'll manage here, won't you?'

'Of course,' Samantha said quickly. It sounded like heaven to her—a full two-and-a-half-day reprieve from his company. After last night she needed one. 'We'll get lots of work done.'

'You can keep the car and do a bit of sightseeing,' Jason said as he folded a stack of multi-coloured T-shirts and stowed them in his duffel. 'Have you seen much of California before, Sam?'

Samantha ignored the 'Sam', knowing he did it merely to annoy her. 'No.'

'Well, Andi will broaden your education this weekend and I'll see what we can do to continue it when I get back.'

'I don't want——'

'But I do,' he said, running roughshod over her objections as usual. Why couldn't he understand she didn't *want* to be anywhere near him? Had Louis Lambert badgered her mother this way? For the first time she began to feel a twinge of sympathy for Margot.

'And don't forget the sun-screen this time.' Jason tapped her nose with his forefinger. 'You still bear a startling resemblance to one of Santa's reindeer.'

Samantha made a face, but she knew he was right, and she certainly wouldn't forget again. His command to 'strip' yesterday, followed by a night spent tossing and turning, as she felt the heat still radiating from her face and neck and the other exposed areas of her body, had convinced her of that.

Jason zipped up the duffel, tucked his airline tickets into the pocket of his polo shirt and parked a pair of sunglasses on his nose. He tossed Samantha the keys. 'Let's go.'

She was glad at least that she'd always been a competent driver. It was, she sometimes felt, her major accomplishment, the one thing she could actually do better than her father. Ambrose didn't drive at all. One couldn't drive in traffic and commune with Bach and Beethoven. So, from the earliest possible age, Samantha had obtained her driver's licence and had chauffeured her father wherever he'd needed to go. She had never driven a Jeep before, but she found the experience oddly exhilarating. The wind whipped through her hair and the cool, slightly overcast morning air was gentle on her sunburnt cheeks.

She even handled the airport traffic with no problem. Jason seemed pleased. 'Good job, Sam. Just follow the signs and head south. You'll be home in no time,' he told her when she pulled up in front of the terminal from which he was to leave. 'See you Sunday night. I'll call when I get in.'

He reached round behind him and grabbed the duffel bag, tossing it to a waiting porter. Then he turned back to Samantha, leaned towards her and kissed her.

She gasped.

'Gotta keep up appearances.' He winked, bounded out, and in moments was gone.

But not forgotten.

As soon as Samantha got back to the house, Andrea said, 'Let's go to Disneyland.'

'Disneyland? Today? Oh, heavens, no,' Samantha protested. 'We can't.'

'Why not? Jason said to sightsee. Why not start with the most popular tourist attraction around?'

'But I'm here to work, not to be a tourist,' Samantha reminded her.

Andrea shrugged. 'We've plenty of time to work. Come on, Samantha *pleeeeeease*. Jason said to.' She looked imploringly at the older girl.

Jason. Jason. Jason. Samantha wished she could plug her ears. 'We really need to work, Andrea.'

'What about if I promise to work like a demon until noon? Then can we go?'

'Noon?'

'That's two whole hours. And I worked four hours yesterday, between your lesson and practising. Don't be a slave-driver, Samantha.'

'I'd hardly call what we did yesterday slavery. We spent the entire afternoon on the beach.' Much to her misfortune, she thought, with a grimace that still made her cheeks tingle.

Andrea just looked up hopefully.

Samantha sighed. 'All right, we'll go. *If* we get busy right now.'

Andrea beamed. 'Great. You'll love Disneyland, Samantha. You'll just love it.'

Amazingly, she did. Ambrose considered Disneyland a variety of juvenile foolishness he couldn't be bothered with, so they never had gone there, not even when they'd had extra time in Los Angeles a few years back. Samantha had told herself it hadn't mattered—there were many more important things in the world to see and do. Disneyland was for children.

But, she discovered the moment she set foot in the Magic Kingdom with Andrea, it was also for adults who had it in them to become children again themselves. Surprisingly, she found that she did.

She was enchanted by everything she saw—by the rides, the life-size Disney cartoon characters, the whole ambience of make-believe that enveloped them as soon as they arrived.

Andrea tugged her from Fantasyland to Adventureland to Frontierland. She cajoled Samantha into swooping down the Matterhorn and to boating through the darkest jungle. The two of them wandered through Injun Joe's cave on Tom Sawyer's Island, sailed over London in Captain Hook's pirate ship, and scaled the tree-house belonging to the Swiss Family Robinson.

And everywhere they went, Andrea said, 'I wish Jason were here.'

To Samantha's way of thinking, he was. The giddy, stomach-churning feeling she had as their bobsled skimmed and swooped its way down the Matterhorn instantly reminded her of the way her stomach had felt when he'd kissed her that morning. The roguish pirates of the Caribbean they passed as they sailed through that ride made her see an equally roguish Jason Cole in her mind's eye. The intrepid guide, wise-cracking his way through the jungle, tossed off remarks with the same arrogant insouciance that Jason did.

He was, Samantha knew, clear across the country. He was—in her mind—wherever she went.

But, in spite of Samantha's preoccupation, she had a wonderful time. They ate supper in a New Orleans-style bistro, then wandered through the shops in Main Street as the sky darkened in the west. Then they leaned against a lamp-post and watched the most spectacular fireworks display Samantha had ever seen in her life.

That reminded her of Jason, too. Small ones seemed to go off whenever she was around him. And the large ones, shooting off into the heavens above her now, made her wonder if other bigger ones lurked undetected in their relationship. And while wisdom told her that yes, they did, and that it was the better part of good sense to leave well enough alone, some perverse part of Samantha was intrigued and attracted by the possibility.

And when the last one exploded in the sky and a rainbow of colours sizzled and scattered, then died, leaving her staring into the blackness, she sighed at the beauty of it and knew that it left her hungry for more.

The drive home was long and tiring. Samantha put on the radio and fiddled with it until she found a classical station. Andrea, who had started out the journey quite chatty, before long leaned her head back and shut her eyes. Within minutes she was asleep. They didn't get in until almost midnight. The phone was ringing when they did.

Samantha was going to simply leave the answering machine to deal with it, until she heard Jason's voice on the other end of the line.

'It's Jason. Again.' Heavy emphasis came down on the last word. 'It's midnight, for goodness' sake. Where the hell are—— ?'

'Hello,' Samantha broke in.

'Thank heaven! Where have you been? Are you all right?'

'We're fine. We——'

'Fine? Then why haven't you answered the phone?'

'We haven't been here.'

'All day?' The palpable relief in his voice seemed to be changing to anger by the second.

'We went to Disneyland.'

'*Disneyland?*' That word was half-yelp, half-thunder.

'You said we should sightsee,' Samantha reminded him. 'And Andrea wanted to go. We did practise all morning first.'

'Disneyland.' The word now was a sigh of relief. 'Cripes, I didn't know what the hell happened to you. I wondered if you'd even made it home from the airport. I've been calling since I got here. At first I figured you must have. Then I wasn't sure.'

'I'm sorry you were worried,' Samantha said, still surprised, trying to mollify him. 'I didn't realise you were planning to call.'

Jason cleared his throat. 'Yeah, well, I thought I should. I am Andrea's guardian and all. And since I'm clear across the country...'

'Of course,' Samantha agreed promptly. 'Well, rest assured, she's fine.'

'Did you like it?' he asked.

'Like what?'

'Disneyland. Did you like it?'

'Oh, yes.' She couldn't help smiling. 'It was lovely.'

'What did you like best?'

'The Pirates of the Caribbean.'

'Why?'

That stopped her. She'd known the answer to Jason's first question at once. She hadn't realised, though, until he'd asked why, that the reason was because one swash-buckling, blue-eyed pirate in particular had reminded her of him.

'It was such fun,' she said lamely. 'I just thought it was beautiful. I felt as if I'd been swept away into another world.'

'I know what you mean.' His voice was softer now, almost dreamy. It reminded Samantha of the lateness of the hour, of the fact that Andrea had shut off her light and gone to bed, that she herself was curled cosily into the corner of the sofa, her shoes off, her head lying against a pillow, and that in Florida it was three o'clock in the morning and Jason must be in bed, too. That last thought made her cheeks warm, and the same slightly giddy feeling she'd come to associate with him took hold of her stomach again.

'I remember the last time I was at Disneyland,' he told her. And he went on, talking about getting dizzy in a teacup and about how he and a friend of his had made the suspension bridge sway so much that no one would get on it. 'It was great fun,' he said. 'Like being a kid again.'

'Yes,' Samantha agreed. She had no trouble imagining Jason as a child.

'I'm glad you got to go,' he said. 'You need a few things like that.'

Another time when she'd been wider awake, more defensive, she might have objected. Tonight she agreed.

'Even if I went crazy today worrying about you,' he added drily.

'Did you try to call often?'

'About twenty times. You can count 'em when you rewind the answering-machine tape.'

'I really am sorry we worried you. I imagine you needed to get to sleep.'

'I needed to know you were all right.'

'We are.' She tried to sound brisk, but she only sounded sleepy.

'Yeah.' There was a pause. 'Samantha?'

'What?'

She could almost hear the smile in his voice as he said quietly, 'Wish you were here.' Then, before she could say a word, she heard the soft buzz of the dialling tone.

Jason, it turned out, had called twenty-two times. Aunt Hortense had called three. And, miracle of miracles, Oliver, too, had rung up.

'Where are you, Samantha?' he said plaintively when she replayed the tape. 'I need to talk to you.' But he hadn't left a number for her to phone him back.

It was just as well, Samantha thought, that she hadn't run back the tape before she went to bed. If she had, she'd have been awake all night trying to decide what it was that Oliver 'needed' to talk to her about. It was quite bad enough that the last words she'd heard before sleeping had been Jason's soft, 'Wish you were here.' It had played havoc with her equanimity for most of the night.

She didn't go down to the beach on Saturday. Andrea wheedled and cajoled her, but in vain. Finally the younger girl went off with the girls with whom she'd gone out Thursday night, leaving Samantha to wait for Oliver's next call. She needed to hear from him. Badly.

He didn't ring. The phone did, of course. And each time Samantha leaped to answer it, but to no avail.

The first five calls were for Jason. Four from breathless-sounding groupies who didn't even leave their names, the fifth from a man who told Samantha that he oversaw Cole Sportwear when Jason was on tour.

'I know he's not there, and I know he doesn't want to hear from me now. He never talks to anyone from Friday until Sunday. It's all tournament with him then. But have him call me first thing Sunday night, the minute he walks in the door. Promise?'

Samantha promised. Odd, she thought as she hung up and went back to her magazine. Jason had talked to her, and he hadn't sounded especially single-minded. In fact, he hadn't mentioned the tournament at all. But then, maybe his concern for Andrea overrode his pre-occupation with volleyball. She wouldn't have thought it, but, if it was true, it was something else about Jason Cole that raised him in her estimation.

The phone rang again as soon as Andrea and the girls went back to the beach after lunch. The voice asking for Jason this time managed to be ponderous and elderly as well as female.

'I'm afraid he isn't available,' Samantha said. 'May I take a message?'

'Off gallivanting at one of those ridiculous games, is he? That you, Andrea?' the bassoon-voice demanded.

'No, ma'am. But——'

'This Miss Peabody, then?'

'Er—yes.'

'Glad to meet you, girl. Very glad,' the voice boomed. 'Hortense Strong here. Andrea's aunt. Heard a lot about you. Tremendous teacher, Andrea says. Taught her heaps. Glad to hear it. Looking forward, in fact, to hearing it. How's Monday?'

'I beg your pardon?' Samantha was still trying to fit in the missing words.

'Want to hear you. How's Monday?'

'Oh—er—that would be fine. Er—just fine.'

'Right. Nine.' The phone thudded in Samantha's ear.

So that was Aunt Hortense. Being domineering was clearly something of a family trait. She wondered what Jason would say when she told him how like his aunt he was!

But before she could speculate, the phone rang again. And this time it was Oliver.

'Sammie Cat?'

'Oliver!'

'Which dry-cleaner did you send my tails to in New York?'

That was what he wanted to ask her?

'Er—the one on Amsterdam, just around the corner from Rudley. Why? Surely you got them back?'

'Of course. But I need them done again, and no one on tour seems to have the slightest notion of how to take care of all that.'

'What? Oliver, there are dry-cleaners in every city in the world.' That might have been a slight exaggeration, but Samantha didn't think so.

'You wouldn't know it,' Oliver grumbled. 'Nobody to take care of things like that.'

I would have, Samantha thought. 'Where are you?'

'I'm in Williamsburg. I thought you knew that.'

He had given Samantha a schedule, but she realised guiltily that she hadn't consulted it since she'd been here. 'Oh, of course. It must have slipped my mind. Sorry.'

'I've lost my gold studs as well,' he went on. 'You did pack them, didn't you?'

'Yes, Oliver.' She'd gone up to Boston and done all his packing before she'd packed herself.

'Hmm. I'm beginning to think I should have brought you along after all.' She heard a half-teasing, half-plaintive note in his voice.

'Yes. Well, you had your chance.'

'Maybe you should come.'

Samantha wasn't sure she'd heard right. 'What? Come out there? Now?'

'I need you, Sammie.'

Oh, lord, why now? Why not a month ago? 'Oliver, I have a job. I can't come now.'

There was an audible snort at the other end of the line. 'Job? It's not really a job, Sammie. Only baby-sitting that Cole girl.'

Samantha sighed. Oliver had, if possible, even less respect for her teaching than her father did.

'Well, I'm committed to her,' she said placatingly, knowing that men like Oliver couldn't be expected to understand what teaching meant to her. 'And anyway, I'm sure you can find a dry-cleaner, Oliver. Check the *Yellow Pages*. Ask someone.'

He gave a long-suffering sigh. 'You won't do it?'

'I *can't* do it, Oliver.'

'You could,' he said sulkily. When she didn't speak, he sighed again. 'I suppose I can manage. It isn't easy, though. Thank heaven for room service at least. But they don't do as good a job as you do with a steak.'

Samantha smiled, glad he was learning to appreciate her. 'I'm flattered.'

'I really do wish you were here, Sammie Cat. You'd love it. A chance to explore new things during the week, concerts every weekend. My Bach piece is getting better and better. You should hear it.'

'I will,' Samantha promised. 'I'll be in the Hamptons, remember?'

'So you will. And thank goodness for that.'

'Yes,' Samantha agreed.

'We'll have a wonderful time,' he said eagerly. 'I promise. And since we've spent the summer apart, I'll have so much to tell you. It'll be wonderful getting reacquainted, won't it? I'm particularly looking forward to reacquainting myself with your lips.'

Samantha blushed guiltily, remembering who had last acquainted himself with her lips.

'Perhaps I can get to know a bit more of you, too,' Oliver insinuated softly.

Samantha shifted uncomfortably. 'Perhaps.'

'Good. Oops. There's . . . someone knocking at my door. Ah, Nell. Must run. *Au revoir,* my love.' And with a speed that rivalled Hortense Strong's, he was gone.

Oliver's phone call was not the panacea she'd hoped it would be. He had certainly done what she'd been wishing he would: asked her to leave California and come to him. But for what reason? Was his 'need' for her simply an extension of finding out the name of the dry-cleaner she habitually used? That was what it sounded like.

She shouldn't be surprised. Oliver hadn't had to deal with much in the real world, not since she had moved down to New York to work at Rudley. Even though he spent a lot of his time in Boston now, she still cooked for him at weekends and got his laundry and dry-cleaning done.

Perhaps this separation really was a good thing, she thought, as she stretched her bare feet out in front of her and contemplated her sunburned toes. Perhaps their being apart would make Oliver really appreciate her. At least, it was to be hoped.

She was just considering that possibility when the phone rang again. This time the feminine voice was more mature than the groupies, but it had enough of the same sultry seductiveness to lift the hairs on the back of Samantha's neck.

'Is Jason there?'

'No, I'm sorry. May I take a message?'

'Tell him Dena called, will you? You must be the cello lady.' There was a soft laugh. 'Jason told me all about you.'

'He did?'

'Oh, yes. He tells me everything.'

'How nice,' Samantha said through her teeth.

'I'd like to meet you.'

Samantha thought she might like to meet Dena Whoever-she-was, too. It would be a good antidote to whatever growing good feeling she'd been developing about her employer.

Leopards don't change their spots, she reminded herself. And neither do arrogant, 'take what they want' businessmen. Remember Fritz. Remember Louis Lambert. Remembering Oliver was somehow not quite enough.

The phone rang once more that night. Samantha was already half asleep when she heard it. The closest one was in Jason's room, and, since it had already rung four times before she got up, that was where she went to answer it.

'I woke you up.' It was Jason. Recognising him sent a tiny shiver down the length of Samantha's spine.

'Yes,' she said with as much crispness as she could muster. He was Dena's, and she wanted nothing to do with him, she reminded herself.

'Sorry.' But he didn't sound it. He sounded pleased, as well as tired and slightly sleepy himself.

Not surprising, since it was after one in the morning there. Had he been out partying and had just got in?

'So, what did you do today?' he asked her.

'Very little. Answered the phone, went to the beach, answered the phone.'

He chuckled softly. 'I've got you trained.'

'You didn't have a thing to do with it,' she informed him. 'Did you want to speak to Andrea?'

'No. I wanted to speak to you.'

'Why?'

'Do any more sightseeing?' he asked, ignoring her question.

'No.'

'Good. We can do it when I get back.'

'That won't be necessary. I'll be teaching Andrea when you get back. And I'm sure you have work to do as well.'

'You know what they say about all work and no play, Sam.'

'My work is my play,' Samantha said firmly.

'Yeah,' he said, surprising her. 'So's mine. I know what you mean.' There was a pause, and she heard him yawn. It was a strangely intimate sound. It sent a shiver down her spine.

'Your aunt called.'

He groaned. 'What did she want?'

'To meet me, it appears. She's going to be dropping by Monday morning. At nine.' At least, she supposed that was what that one-word utterance meant.

'Nine?' Jason howled. 'She knows I sleep in on Mondays.'

'She wants to meet me, not you.'

'Doesn't matter. She'll expect me to be up and standing at attention.'

Samantha smiled in spite of herself. 'Yes, I can see how she might. She sounds a bit formidable.'

'She *is* a bit formidable.' He sighed. 'Great. Now I can look forward to that all weekend.'

'I have something better for you to look forward to,' Samantha told him. 'Your girlfriend called, too. She wants you to call her on Monday as well.'

'Girlfriend?'

Did he have so many he didn't know which one she was talking about? 'She said her name was Dena.'

'Dena called?' There was a sudden note of urgency in his voice. 'How is she?'

'She sounded just fine,' Samantha said flatly. 'Why?'

'No reason. She's . . . been a bit under the weather. Where was she?'

'How should I know?'

Jason sighed. 'She didn't say?'

'No. She said for you to call her Monday, that she had to leave town on Tuesday. Nothing much.' She certainly was not going to tell him what Dena had said about what good friends they were, and how they told each other everything.

'OK. Thanks.'

Samantha waited for him to say goodbye and hang up, as everyone else had, but he didn't. She could hear the soft sound of his breathing above the hum of the long-distance connection.

'What's the weather like?' he asked.

'The weather? Cloudy. Why? Shouldn't you be sleeping?'

'Yeah, probably. But I'd rather talk to you. Was it foggy today? Sunny? How was the surf?'

Samantha felt the shiver come back. 'Overcast in the morning,' she told him, trying to sound businesslike, but not really managing. She was too sleepy. She settled back against the pillows on the headboard of his bed and tucked her feet under her.

'It was sunny here,' he said. 'Hot, too.'

'Not here. It barely made seventy-five.'

'I'd love it.'

It was a pointless conversation. Small talk. Barely better than gibberish. But Jason seemed in no hurry to end it. Yawning, Samantha leaned her head against the pillows and kept answering his questions, oddly reluctant to end it, either.

It was soothing, somehow, talking about the weather, about the waves, about how Andrea was doing on her cello, about whether Samantha's sunburn was better. This last question left her slightly less soothed, but he only asked conversationally, so she answered easily enough.

'It's getting much better. I've been putting the ointment on it.'

'Did you put on sun-screen before you went out in the sun today?'

'Yes.'

She heard a soft sigh, and she thought he smiled. 'Wish I'd been there to put it on for you.'

Samantha sat bolt upright. 'I don't need anyone to put it on for me.'

'Need isn't the issue, Sam,' he said softly. 'It's want. And there's not much I want more than sliding my hands all over you.'

'Jason!' Untucking her feet, she slapped them down flat on the hardwood floor.

'It's true.'

'Stop it. Don't say things like that!' She scrambled off his bed and glared at the phone in the dark.

'Why not? Does the truth make you tremble, Sam? It does me.'

With a whimper of outrage, she banged the phone in his ear. Then she stood shivering in the faint gleam of moonlight, hugging herself and—damn him—yes, trembling.

When she crawled back into her own bed minutes later, she lay staring up at the ceiling, thinking about the man she had just hung up on. He seemed to have an uncanny ability to weasel past her defences, to slip in on her weakest side, and then, just when she was most vulnerable, to swoop down upon her and provoke a reaction. The way he combined forcefulness and gentleness completely baffled her. It wasn't what she expected at all. She'd been too young to know how Louis had tempted away her mother, but she'd had her own experience with Fritz. He'd swept her off her feet, plied her with compliments and promises all designed to get what he'd wanted. Jason seemed as willing to provoke and to tease as to tempt.

But if in that way he was different—read, more subtle—than Louis Lambert or Fritz Hoffmann, she had to remind herself that that didn't mean the end result of his campaign would be any different.

Oh, in one case it would—Louis had at least married her mother. But Fritz had never intended to marry her, for all his promises, and Ambrose had made sure she'd known it. Samantha knew Jason had no intentions of marrying her either. If he married anyone it would undoubtedly be the breathless Dena.

In the meantime he would do his best to get what he wanted. And the end result would be even worse. Not just because, once Jason had had her, he would leave her and take her self-respect with him, but most of all because, if she wasn't careful, she suspected that he could make her fall in love with him as well.

CHAPTER FIVE

'AUNT HORTENSE is coming here? Today?' Andrea moved from sound sleep to clearly horrified wakefulness in scant seconds.

'At nine o'clock,' Samantha said briskly. 'So you'd better get a move on. She'll be here in less than an hour.'

'Oh, lord! She can't! Samantha, wait!' Andrea flung back the covers and leaped to her feet.

Samantha turned. 'What?'

'I'm ill.' Andrea sank back down. She did look suddenly pale, Samantha thought. But she certainly had been sleeping well and soundly moments before. 'I'm nauseated. My stomach hurts.'

'This wouldn't have anything to do with Aunt Hortense, would it?' Samantha asked drily. 'I wouldn't let her worry me, if I were you. It's not you she's checking out—it's me.'

'That's the problem,' Andrea said. 'I mean... Oh, my stomach.'

Samantha turned on her heel and came to stand over the bed. 'What's the problem?' she asked, hearing ominous things in the words Andrea had just uttered.

'I... Really, Samantha, why don't you just call her and tell her we can't possibly see her today? Tell her we'll call her when it's convenient. When I'm feeling better.'

Samantha sat down on the edge of the bed. 'Just exactly what is it about Aunt Hortense's visit that's making you sick?'

Andrea stared out the window, not meeting Samantha's eyes. Her fingers plucked worriedly at the quilt. 'She's going to have a fit,' she said at last.

'A fit? And why would she have a fit?'

More worried plucking. A heartfelt sigh. 'Because of what she thinks.'

'What does she think?'

Andrea thumped her fist on the bed. 'It's so stupid. I mean, I ought to know what's best for me, oughtn't I?'

Samantha wasn't quite sure she followed this particular twist in the conversation, but she figured that its occurrence indicated that they were coming close to the heart of the problem. 'What does she think?'

Andrea rolled on to her side, still staring away from Samantha as she said tonelessly, 'She thinks you're fifty.'

'What?'

'Well, not quite fifty. But older than you are.'

'But why? And what difference does it make? And——'

'Exactly,' Andrea wailed. 'What difference does it make? That's what I'd like to know. But when I knew I was coming to stay here with Jason this year, she insisted on some old biddy to come with me on tour. I wanted you.'

The last words were said softly but firmly, and Samantha was glad she was sitting down because she felt suddenly weak. 'Oh, dear.'

'Yeah,' Andrea said glumly. 'So now will you call her and tell her not to come?'

'I don't see how I can do that, Andrea. She's probably on her way. And even if she weren't,' Samantha added, 'I wouldn't want to lie to her.'

'Well, what are we going to do?'

'What's the matter?' Jason loomed in the doorway. Samantha felt a quickening at the sight of him. She had counselled herself on aloofness again all day Sunday, but just seeing him when she'd picked him up at the airport last night had made hash of that notion. She found herself in the same predicament today.

He looked as if he'd just got up, his sun-gilded hair tousled and whiskery stubble covering his jaw. But even that way—particularly that way—he made Samantha's heart go from *allegro* to *presto* in her chest.

'What's going on?' Jason asked again.

Andrea looked down. 'Aunt Hortense thinks Samantha is about fifty,' she mumbled.

'Fifty?' Jason just stared at her. Then he wiped a hand over his face and stared harder. His gaze shifted to Samantha, raking her with such hungry thoroughness that she felt as if she'd been stripped. There was a short bark of disbelieving laughter. 'You told Hortense she was fifty?'

'She wanted her to be fifty,' Andrea said sullenly.

Jason grabbed the door-jamb for support. 'Oh, cripes,' he moaned. 'And you know what she'll think, don't you?'

'What?' Andrea and Samantha asked together.

'That I put you up to it. That Samantha is my latest...' He had the grace to blush.

If Samantha hadn't been the 'latest' in question, she might have sympathised with Aunt Hortense.

Jason managed a grin, his eyes still caressing as much of her figure as he could see beneath the full skirt and long-sleeved blouse. 'Not that I don't think it's a good idea.'

Samantha glowered at him. So did Andrea.

'That's not helping, Jason,' the younger girl said. 'She'll make me go live with her, and you know it.'

He sobered at once. 'No, she won't.'

'She will, if she finds out about Samantha. You know she has to give her approval.'

'What approval?' Samantha wanted to know.

'Andi's mother didn't want me burdened——' Jason grimaced even as he said the word '—with the task of raising Andi alone if I didn't want to, so her will gave Hortense and me equal custody until Andi's eighteen. She gets to be with me in the first instance, that's stated. But Hortense can make stipulations about her living arrangements. And if I don't want her, or if Hortense perceives "problems"——' another grimace '—then she can ask for custody.'

'And you think she's going to?'

'Hortense has a veritable gift for perceiving problems.' Jason shook his head. His knuckles whitened as he gripped the door-jamb. 'My lifestyle. My occupation. My friends. You name it.'

'Your women?' Samantha suggested.

Jason gave her a hard look.

'So you think she wants Andrea?'

'She wants the control that goes with having Andrea, I know that. If she gets custody, she'll have control of all of Andi's mother's shares. It'll give her that much more clout on the board.'

'And if you have Andrea,' Samantha pointed out, 'you'll have control.'

'I already own fifty percent of the stock now,' Jason snapped, the first genuine anger she'd seen from him flashing in his eyes. 'I can do what I want. All it means is that Hortense can wield a slightly bigger stick. She still won't knock me out with it. I care about Andrea! Nothing more, nothing less.'

Samantha swallowed. Even she couldn't doubt the sincerity in that remark. 'I'm sorry.'

'Don't be.' He flashed her a devastating grin. 'As I said, I rather like the idea.'

Samantha's jaw snapped shut. 'Stop that! Stop it right now. We have to think. She's going to be here in less than forty minutes.'

'You mean you'll help?' Both Andrea and Jason seemed surprised.

Samantha just looked at both of them. 'Of course.'

Forty-two minutes later, when Aunt Hortense's heavy tread crossed the porch, Samantha and Andrea were in the midst of a Bach duet.

'We can't disturb them right now,' Samantha heard Jason say, arresting Hortense's progress right outside the window. 'Big mistake to interrupt their concentration. But, of course,' he went right on over her incipient protest, 'as a cellist yourself, you know that.'

Hortense Strong had never been more than a middling cellist at best, but she was never one to point that out. She took great pride in being a role model for Andrea, and Jason knew it.

'Indeed.' She paused, considered, then nodded her agreement as she squinted through the window-screen. 'Suspect you're right. And I can hear just as well from here.'

'Of course. You can get a better idea, in fact,' Jason said, while Samantha prayed he wouldn't overdo it. 'They're more comfortable on their own, you know.'

'Quite.'

Andrea sawed gamely away, carrying the melody, while Samantha backed her up, bending her head and praying that through the screen the faint dusting of talcum powder on her hair looked like the streaks of grey she had intended.

They'd pinned her hair up into a bun, then Andrea had brushed the powder on to it. It wasn't a professional make-up job, but last autumn, when the Rudley School had done *Arsenic and Old Lace*, Samantha had been pressed into helping out with make-up and she'd learned a fair bit. Enough, she hoped, to at least mislead Aunt Hortense. It wasn't lying, she told herself, merely acting.

At least she hoped that, come Judgement Day, that was all it was.

Jason had frowned all the time he'd watched Andrea streak the hair. 'If she doesn't look too closely, I guess we might get away with it. The clothes are right, at least.'

It hadn't been a compliment, and Samantha had known it. He didn't like her full skirts and demure blouses. But she wore them anyway. It was a matter of principle.

So when Jason had offered her an old cardigan of his father's, saying, 'It goes with the outfit,' wordlessly she had put it on, pushing the sleeves up so they wouldn't tangle in the strings of her cello.

'Not the shoes, though,' Jason had decreed.

'What's wrong with my shoes?' Samantha wore her sandals everywhere. 'I may not be fifty, but at least these are sensible shoes.'

'For herding water buffalo, maybe. They don't fit the strait-laced biddy image we need to create.'

He'd rummaged through her suitcase and Andrea's, finally coming up with a pair of Andrea's tennis shoes, three sizes too big, which he'd handed to her.

'I'll trip.'

'Don't walk. Just sit, play the cello, and between movements look as if your rheumatism bothers you. I'll do the rest.'

So Samantha had stuffed her feet into the shoes, picked up her bow and, when Aunt Hortense had lumbered up the steps a quarter of an hour later, they'd begun to play.

It was, thank heavens, a long piece. Very baroque, with lots of counterpoint and codswallop, with a hundred or so repetitions and variations thrown in. It wouldn't matter, then, Samantha decided, if they added another twenty more to stretch things out should they need to.

She and Andrea played on all the while Aunt Hortense and Jason talked. They stood on the porch and talked,

they sat on the porch and talked. Then Jason paced while
Aunt Hortense sat and continued to talk.

'Dedicated, I can tell,' Samantha heard Aunt Hortense
say, peering in the window at her once more. 'Quite determined. You can see it in the chin.'

'Yes, indeed,' came Jason's reply. 'Very much so.
Formidable.'

'Sure she's healthy? Looks a bit frail from here,' Aunt
Hortense mused. 'Know I specified an older woman, but
is she spry enough to handle a girl Andrea's age?'

'She's swifter on her feet than she looks,' Jason said
easily, making Samantha struggle to keep a straight face.
'For an old gal she really gets around.'

'Very strict, is she?'

'Oh, absolutely. A regular Tartar.'

'Andrea does seem to be thriving.' This last was
grudging.

'I was sure you'd think so.' Jason almost managed
not to sound smug.

Aunt Hortense hoisted herself slowly to her feet. 'Like
to speak to her though, find out what her plans are.
Think they'll be stopping soon?'

'I doubt it. Quite a taskmaster is our Ms Peabody.
They practise all morning. Starting at dawn.'

'You'd do well to learn from her.' Aunt Hortense
sniffed.

'Oh, I do,' Samantha heard Jason reply.

Aunt Hortense appeared speechless for a moment.
Then, 'Can't wait forever,' she grumbled. 'See her again
another day. Want to tell her about when we played the
Breval when I was young.'

'I'll have her call you,' Jason offered, beginning to
herd Hortense towards the steps.

'Do that,' Aunt Hortense instructed. 'I expect to be
kept abreast, Jason.' She turned and tapped his bare
chest with a plump finger. 'For the time being I find
things are at least reasonably in hand. But vigilance is

all. And I shall be vigilant, never fear. Owe it to Andrea's dear mother.' So saying, she clumped down the steps and disappeared around the corner of the house.

Andrea's playing flagged momentarily.

'Again.' Samantha, unwilling to stop until the coast was absolutely clear, launched into the forty-eighth variation, and, after a moment, Andrea followed.

Jason waited until Aunt Hortense had safely vanished, then appeared in the doorway and gave them the thumbs up sign. 'Right,' he said jubilantly. 'Now, how about a swim?'

'Super,' Andrea said and set her bow aside.

'Not on your life,' Samantha said. 'We're working.'

'But——'

'Working. We're practising all morning,' Samantha reminded her. 'Isn't that what your brother said? Starting at dawn?'

'But——'

'We didn't start at dawn, though,' Samantha went on implacably. 'So we'd better make up for it now.'

Andrea looked from Jason to Samantha, then back again. Jason shrugged and gave her a wink. 'Work hard, Andi. See you later.' Then he picked up a beach towel and a volleyball off the sofa and headed for the door, whistling.

Only when he started down the steps did he look back at his sister. 'When you do come down, don't forget the sun-screen. Especially you, Sam.'

'My name's not Sam!' Samantha snapped at his back, but he just gave her a cheeky wave and loped off towards the volleyball courts down at the beach.

'He likes you,' Andrea informed her happily.

Samantha snorted. She appealed to Jason Cole the way the three little pigs appealed to the big bad wolf. She got out the concerto they were really working on. 'Start at the top of page three. We need to work on your phrasing. I'll just go and change.'

The lesson went well. At least, as well as it could be expected to go when Jason and three similar specimens interrupted it periodically to raid the refrigerator and then to stand, staring and commenting, while Samantha instructed Andrea in a particularly difficult set of harmonics.

Samantha thought Jason might have allowed it simply to annoy her. It seemed the sort of thing he'd do. But, oddly, he seemed to want to ignore the two girls as much as Samantha wanted to ignore him. It wasn't easy for either of them.

'Who's she?' one man whispered loudly to Jason, nodding his head at Samantha as he craned his neck to watch from the kitchen.

'Who're *they*?' another demanded, obviously with an eye to both Samantha and Andrea.

'Who cares? I'll take 'em whoever they are,' said the third with a lascivious grin. He smacked his lips.

'The blonde's my sister,' Jason said sharply, letting the refrigerator door bang shut. 'And the other one's mine. Hands off.'

She was *his*? Said who? Samantha's head jerked around to glare at him. He had the audacity to give her a blatant wink. She bristled, about to retort that she most certainly was not his, when she took a good look at the men with him.

Also tall, also hunky, also muscular and displaying an inordinate amount of tanned, firm, masculine flesh, they could have been clones of Jason Cole except for one thing. They had even more lust in their eyes than he did.

Samantha swallowed hard and turned quickly back to her music. 'From the beginning,' she said to Andrea determinedly.

'But you said——'

'From the beginning.' Samantha's tone brooked no argument.

Andrea sighed, shot a covert glance and small smile in the direction of the youngest and blondest of Jason's cohorts, and reluctantly began the Bach piece again.

'Let's go,' Jason said abruptly when the other three showed decided reluctance about heading for the door. 'We've got work to do.'

'Hey, Jase——' one protested.

'Let's go.'

'But——' began the tallest one.

'Hey, man, we just want a couple more minutes,' protested another. 'A little course in music appreciation, y'know.'

'Come on.' It wasn't a suggestion this time, but an order. Jason herded them past, almost shoving when they lingered, listening.

Then, just when Samantha felt like crowing, 'Free! Free, at last!' as he edged them towards the door, he bent and dropped a kiss on her hair as he slipped quickly past. 'Carry on, Sam.'

Samantha's face flamed. Her playing went suddenly flat.

'They're not bad,' she heard the young, blond one, who was still looking over his shoulder, say to Jason as they reached the door. 'Do you s'pose they can play Springsteen?'

'I am not yours.' Samantha confronted Jason that evening in the kitchen. She had held her tongue all during dinner, all during the washing-up that the three of them had shared. But now Andrea had gone off with her girlfriends again, and Samantha felt she had to straighten things out.

'No?' Jason gave her a mocking grin.

'No!' Her cheeks burned. 'And you needn't pretend I am.'

'Would you rather fend them off yourself, sweetheart?' he asked, his grin broadening.

She looked down her nose at him. 'It wouldn't come to that.'

'Don't count on it. You're desirable as hell. Even with those ridiculous clothes.' He gave a scathing look to the skirt and blouse she'd worn to deceive Aunt Hortense and which she still wore.

'They're not ridiculous,' she retorted. 'They're very suitable.'

'For playing the cello or gathering rosebuds maybe. They don't do much on the beach.'

'They're fine,' Samantha argued. In fact, they weren't. She'd seen that almost at once. But she had been loath to give them up. They were symbolic somehow; they served to remind her of the sort of life she wanted, the values she upheld. And she seemed to need all the help she could get to hold herself apart from the life of Jason Cole and the Southern California crowd.

Privately, of course, she acknowledged that they were death on the beach. The sea breezes were forever whipping her skirt up. And when she caught it between her knees and tried to walk that way, she looked foolish in the extreme. Not to mention that the sand caught in her skirt and in the folds of her blouse, chafing her sunburned skin.

Still, she wouldn't change. She didn't dare.

'I meant to thank you earlier,' he said, leaning back against the refrigerator, his hands tucked into the pockets of his shorts. 'You were a sport.'

'I beg your pardon?'

'With Hortense. I'd compliment you on the act, but sometimes I don't think you mean it as an act.'

Samantha scowled at him. 'What's that supposed to mean?'

'The clothes. The attitude. Sometimes I think you want to be fifty.'

'I do not!'

'Then why persist in dressing that way? In looking down your nose at me like some disapproving nanny?'

'Because you act like you need one.'

Jason's eyebrows lifted. 'Oh? Well, pardon me. You want adult? How's this for adult?' He closed the space between them and took her in his arms.

Samantha tried to shove him away, but he didn't let go. He drew her against him, moulded her curves to his hard lines, let her feel the heat and need in him. She struggled.

'It only makes it worse, Sam.'

'Damn you!'

'It is an act, Samantha, isn't it?'

She stilled in his arms, but he didn't release her, so she gave an experimental tug—to no avail.

Jason's face was scant inches from her own. She could feel the warmth of his breath against her cheek, see the tic of the pulse at the base of his throat. Her own began to race. She shrank back against the counter.

'Isn't it?' His voice was soft, but the softness was a deception.

'Please——'

'Please?' His mouth curved into a smile. 'Why, thank you. Don't mind if I do. I thought you'd never ask.'

Then his lips closed over hers.

This kiss was nothing like the smacking one he'd given her in the restaurant or the fleeting brush of his lips he'd pressed on her outside the airport. The sheer shock of it took her breath away, and the persuasive movement of his lips against her own set her heart into a frantic, staccato beat. It was everything she'd ever imagined a kiss could be and, until now, had never known. It was sweetness, warmth, desire and passion.

It was also Jason Cole!

Samantha gulped, gasped, panicked and, at last, shoved him away.

But not before Jason had proved precisely what he'd set out to prove—what they both knew—that her indifference was only a sham.

'I'm in love,' Andrea announced, flinging herself down on to Samantha's bed.

They were not words Samantha wanted to hear. She continued marking in the alternate fingers on the Saint-Saens concerto. 'Oh, yes?'

Andrea rolled over on to her back and threw her arms wide to embrace the world. 'Yes.'

It was the most emphatically theatrical 'yes' Samantha had ever heard and, coming from Andrea, she found it faintly alarming. She had enough problems with inappropriate love in her own life these days; the feelings that Jason evoked in her—lust, she told herself—still, under whatever name—left her in an emotional tangle. She didn't know what she'd do if she had Andrea to contend with as well. She laid aside her pencil.

'With whom?' she asked cautiously.

'Toby, of course.' Andrea flashed her an impatient look. 'You know.'

Samantha did, now. Toby was the young blond, the one who thought they should play Springsteen, the one who was currently Jason's doubles partner, his regular one having broken a leg skiing at Tahoe last March.

Younger than the rest—whom Samantha had met hanging around the house in the three weeks she'd now been here—at maybe nineteen or twenty, Toby Henning had been introduced to her as Jason's protégé. 'The heir apparent to the kingdom of professional beach volleyball,' one magazine had called him.

The 'heir apparent' hung around a lot. On the porch. In the living-room. In the kitchen. Smiling, chatting, spinning volleyballs on the tip of his finger. Whenever and wherever Samantha turned around, Toby was underfoot.

Just recently, though, she had begun to get the notion that he wasn't hanging about solely out of hero worship for Jason. His gaze was rarely focused on his partner; it was always on Andrea. He seemed, Samantha was beginning to realise, to be as smitten with Andrea as she was now confessing to being with him.

'Oh, dear.'

'What's wrong?' Andrea looked at Samantha curiously.

'Nothing,' Samantha said hastily. She bent over the sheet music while she tried to decide what to do or say next.

Her first inclination was to forbid Andrea to have anything to do with Toby Henning. She was only fifteen, for goodness' sake. A mere child. A baby.

But Andrea didn't have the body of a baby. Her bikini made that all too evident. And she wasn't thinking the thoughts of a baby either.

'Do you think he likes me?' Andrea asked her, her blue eyes wide and anxious.

'Who?'

A groan. 'Toby!'

'Oh. Well, of course he likes you,' Samantha said dismissively. 'What's there not to like?'

'Samanthaaaaaa.'

Samantha felt like wringing her hands. It was one thing to be a chaperon to a girl who spent her life worried about the fingerings of the concerto she was working on. It was going to be quite another to be chaperon to a girl who couldn't get a man off her mind.

What did Samantha know about boy-crazy females? She'd certainly never been one—until now. And her own ill-advised infatuation with Andrea's brother hardly qualified her to chaperon and counsel a besotted young girl.

But if she couldn't, who would? Jason?

There's a laugh, she thought. With the harem of female hangers-on that he attracted on the beach, not to mention the daily phone calls from Dena McGarvey, he'd doubtless be on Toby's side one hundred per cent. After all, what man didn't like to have a woman drooling over him?

'He admires your dedication,' she said to Andrea.

'He what?' Andrea rolled on to her side and propped her head on her bent arm.

'He likes to listen when you play.'

Andrea wrinkled her nose, obviously less than thrilled. 'You think that's all he likes?'

'That isn't enough?'

'Maybe for you,' Andrea conceded. 'With somebody like Oliver. But Toby's not like Oliver.'

Samantha bristled, but she managed a calm, 'No.' Toby was, they both knew, an incipient Jason.

'Do you think he'd like to kiss me?'

'Oliver?'

'Be serious, Samantha. Do you think Toby Henning would like to touch his lips to mine?'

Equanimity vanishing, Samantha snapped her pencil point on the desk. 'What?'

Andrea rolled her eyes. 'Kiss. You know, what people do when they like each other.'

What Jason had done to her. Only he hadn't done it because he liked her. Not really. He'd done it to annoy, to tease, and, most likely, because he thought he could have his way with her. Annoyed, Samantha shoved the memory away.

'I suppose he might,' she allowed, because her conscience wouldn't let her lie outright and say no.

Andrea smiled. A plotting smile. A cunning smile. A womanly smile.

Samantha shuddered at the thought of what was likely going through the young girl's mind. 'Which is not to say you should encourage him,' she said sharply.

'But——'

'Men have only one thing on their minds.'

'Sex?' Andrea said hopefully.

'Andrea!'

'Well?'

'Well, you don't have to sound so thrilled by the idea.'

Andrea gave her a look of total innocence. 'Me?'

Samantha sighed. 'We have work to do. I'd like you to take a look at this music.'

Andrea looked pained. 'But——'

'I agreed to come as your teacher expecting to be able to teach you, not to have to persuade you,' Samantha said firmly. 'I expected a co-operative student. Like the one I had at Rudley.'

'Toby wasn't at Rudley.'

'Thank heavens.' She rattled the sheet of paper at Andrea.

The girl gave a long-suffering groan, then held out her hand. 'All right. But only if we can go swimming after.'

'*You* can go swimming after.'

'No. Both of us.'

'I don't want to swim.'

'And I don't want to practise.'

Samantha gave Andrea a steely glare. Andrea stared back, impassive, her eyes calm but challenging, and the colour of the deep blue sea. Cole eyes. Exactly like Jason's.

Involuntarily, Samantha shivered.

'Just get your toes wet, Sam,' Andrea pleaded.

'I don't want my toes wet,' Samantha said sharply. 'And my name's not Sam!'

'Sure it is,' said a masculine voice from her bedroom doorway, and she looked up to see Jason standing there.

She'd managed to steer clear of him for the last week and a half—ever since the night he'd kissed her in the kitchen. Oh, they'd had the occasional meal together, passed each other in the hallway, and Samantha had no-

ticed Jason lurking about in the background now and
then while she'd been teaching, but she'd deliberately
prolonged the lesson until he'd tired of hanging about
and had gone away.

Now, though, there was no escaping him. He was
leaning barechested against the door-jamb, propping
himself up with an elbow, a grin on his face. The grin
told her that Samantha-baiting was the order of the day.

She gave him a hard look and didn't reply.

'Go take a swim,' he said to his sister.

'We were just going to go over this music,' Samantha
said, to get Andrea to stay without actually contra-
dicting Jason.

'You can do that later,' Jason said.

'But——'

'Later.' Jason's tone brooked no argument. 'I've got
to go to a board meeting in half an hour. You can play
teacher then.'

'I do not "play" teacher.'

He raked fingers through his hair. 'Sorry. No, of
course you don't. I didn't mean that. Go on,' he said
this last to Andrea.

Mystified, shrugging, but obviously glad of the reprieve, Andrea left.

'I brought you something,' Jason said to Samantha.

Her steely look changed to one of wariness. 'Brought
me something? What?'

'My, aren't you suspicious?'

She was. Gifts from Jason Cole had all the potential
of the Trojan Horse. 'Sorry,' she said in a tone that belied
the word. 'What did you bring?'

He turned and lifted a box off the table just outside
her door. 'These.' He put the box in her arms.

It was full of clothes. Shorts and T-shirts in a rainbow
of colours. Bathing-suits. Casual skirts. Several pairs of
faded chambray trousers. A couple of campy-looking
canvas jackets. All brand-new. All bearing tags that pro-

claimed, in bright blue, green and purple letters, NetWork.

'I don't wa——'

'You don't want them. I know that. But you've got them. And I expect you to wear them.' He sounded as if he were talking to a balky child.

'I don't have to wear what you tell me——'

'You do.' He set the box on her bed and pulled a piece of paper out of his pocket. Unfolding it, he read aloud, '"As chaperon and companion to Miss Cole, the employee will co-operate with the wishes of the employer and behave as he deems in the best interests of Miss Andrea Cole."' He lifted his eyes and met hers levelly. 'And I deem it in Andrea's best interests that you wear these clothes.'

'*Andrea's* best interests?' Rage warred with indignation in Samantha's voice.

Jason shrugged. 'Yours, too, for that matter. But I imagine you're too pig-headed to admit that.'

'I don't want——'

'You've said that already.' He faced her squarely. 'Look, Samantha, I've watched you trudging down the beach, your skirt clutched desperately between your knees. I've seen you scratching. *Wear the damned clothes.*'

Samantha went crimson under his penetrating gaze, but he didn't seem to be mocking now. He looked utterly serious, almost concerned.

'Thank you for thinking of me, but I'm fine, really. I'm perfectly comfortable——'

'What you are is a liar, Samantha Peabody,' he said smoothly. 'I thought I proved that the night in the kitchen.'

Her flush deepened.

He went right on, 'Anyway, you don't have a choice. You're wearing these clothes on my orders. Consider it your uniform, if you must.'

'My *uniform*?'

'Lots of nannies have them.'

'Nanny?' Samantha choked. 'Andrea will be horrified.'

'Andrea will be delighted that you've come to your senses at last. She'll be thrilled to have you looking like you belong for a change. Besides,' he added, his tone changing slightly, 'I need you to wear them.'

Her eyes jerked up to meet his. 'Why?'

'We're going to Florida on Friday. When we're at tournaments we wear NetWork clothes, Toby and I. So will Andrea. And so will you. It's the best advertisement we've got—being seen.'

Samantha studied his expression, trying to guess whether he was putting her on or not. He seemed perfectly serious, intent almost.

But she had to try one last time. 'I suppose you'll fire me if I don't.'

Jason just looked at her, his blue eyes clouded and unreadable. Far off she heard the honk of a horn, the roar of a motorcycle as it raced along the alley.

'I think you know the answer to that, Samantha,' he said quietly. And without another word, Jason walked out of the room.

CHAPTER SIX

THE clothes—which she wore and actually enjoyed once Jason's smiles and smirks abated—were the least of Samantha's worries.

The biggest was Andrea. Or, more precisely, Andrea and Toby. It took Andrea less than three days to find out whether Toby liked the idea of kissing her. The answer, both she and Samantha discovered, was emphatically yes. But the fact that Samantha, coming in from a walk, found them locked in each other's arms in the hallway did little for anyone's emotional well-being.

Toby jerked back hastily at Samantha's gasp. His face, always ruddy, flamed now. 'I was just...er—I only...I didn't mean...'

'I'm sure you didn't,' Samantha said frostily. 'I think a nice cold swim would be in order, don't you?'

'Er—yeah.' And Toby fled without a backward glance.

'How could you?' Andrea flared at her the moment they were alone.

'How could I not? It's what I'm being paid for.' Samantha brushed past, trying to sound matter-of-fact and unruffled, trying to squelch the memory of Jason's kiss that had taken place not many steps away, a kiss that had had a similarly devastating effect on her.

'You're being paid to ruin my life?'

'*Ruin your life?* Oh, good heavens!'

'You are! What must Toby think? That I'm a child!'

'You are a child.'

91

'I'm fifteen and I'm in love with him,' Andrea said fervently. 'I told you that. And you act like he's Jack the Ripper.'

'Not quite,' Samantha said drily, following Andrea into her room. 'I'm merely acting responsibly. You're only fifteen, Andrea. Toby is almost twenty. He's an adult.'

'He's only four years older than I am. Jason's seven years older than you.'

Samantha spun around. 'What does Jason have to do with this?'

'I've seen the way he looks at you. And,' Andrea added, 'the way you look at him.'

Samantha glared. 'Utter nonsense.' And anyway, Jason was out with Dena McGarvey at this very moment.

'It isn't. And I'm mortified.' Andrea glowered. 'We weren't doing anything.'

Samantha's eyebrows lifted a fraction of an inch.

Andrea's cheeks flushed guiltily. 'Only kissing.'

'Mmm.'

'That's not so much.'

'Kisses can lead to other things,' Samantha informed the younger girl loftily. 'They can incite your senses.' As well she knew.

'What if I want my senses incited?'

'Andrea!'

Andrea's jaw thrust out. 'Well, what if I do?'

'That's quite enough. You don't need your senses incited. Nor does Toby. Why don't you call one of your girlfriends?' A change of scene—of interest—sounded like a terrific idea.

'You mean you're not going to make me practise another three hours tonight?' Andrea flounced on to her bed, still sulking.

Samantha gave her a hurt look. 'When have I ever done that?'

Andrea had the grace to look ashamed. 'Well, you haven't. But you're being so...strict. You don't know what it's like.'

Didn't she? Samantha feared she was getting a very good idea.

She should have gone to bed hours ago. What point was there, she asked herself again and again, waiting up to discuss Andrea with Jason? Chances were he would be in no shape or mood to discuss anything after a long evening in the company of the estimable Dena McGarvey. But, perversely, she couldn't convince herself to go to bed.

So she sat, flipping through magazines, writing letters to Oliver and her father, watching the late show and then the late, late show. Fretting about Andrea. About Toby. And, to be honest, about Jason.

How foolish was that? she asked herself. He certainly wasn't fretting—or even thinking—about her. He'd got a call from Dena right after he'd got home from a board meeting and, instead of watching a videotape of last week's tournament, which he'd told Samantha he intended to do, she'd heard him say, 'No sweat, sweetheart, I'll be right over,' and he hadn't even bothered to change out of his suit.

He'd paused on his way out the door only long enough to ruffle Samantha's hair. 'Don't wait up,' he'd said cheekily, knowing how to annoy her, knowing that she never would.

And now, idiot that she was, she had.

But she needed to talk to Jason before they left for Florida in the morning, because then her teaching would take a back seat and her 'chaperoning' function would come into greater play. If she was going to do a good job, she needed to have Jason's backing for keeping Andrea on that 'straight and narrow' he'd earlier prescribed.

Tackling him, though, was a task she didn't relish, especially tonight, but she had taken the job and she intended to do it right. That she was curious to see what sort of shape he was in when he returned from his night out with Dena had absolutely nothing to do with it.

It was two-thirty in the morning when the door opened at last. Samantha had fallen asleep on the sofa, waiting, but the sound of the latch woke her and she sat up, yawning and stretching. Jason did a double take when he saw her, and another when she glanced pointedly at her watch.

'Did I miss curfew, then?' A grin tilted one corner of his mouth.

Samantha scowled at him. 'Funny.'

'Well, if I didn't, why are you still sitting up glowering at me?'

'We have something to discuss.'

'That sounds ominous. What happened? Did Hortense show up?' For the first time he sounded concerned.

'No. It has nothing to do with Hortense. It's . . . about Andrea.'

'What about Andrea?' He stripped off the tie he had been wearing and tossed it on to the rocking-chair, then began unbuttoning his shirt. Samantha immediately looked away. What was there about Jason that seemed to require that he be forever stripping off as many clothes as he possibly could? Did he do it around Dena? Stupid question.

'What about Andrea?' he repeated, kicking off his shoes. 'Was she hurt? Did something happen to her?'

'No. At least, not yet.'

The shirt followed the tie on to the rocking-chair. He bent to strip off his socks. 'What do you mean, not yet?'

Samantha took a deep breath. 'I mean, you'd better keep an eye on Toby.'

'Toby? I thought we were talking about Andrea.'

Samantha rolled her eyes. 'We are talking about Andrea. And when one talks about Andrea these days, one must, perforce, talk about Toby.'

'Speak English, why don't you?' Jason suggested. He dropped on to the sofa beside her and stuck his bare feet up on the coffee-table and turned to smile into her eyes. Samantha edged quickly away.

'Want a beer? A glass of brandy?' he asked her.

'No, thank you.' She wanted him to move away. It felt as if he were breathing down her neck.

Jason shrugged and waited, looking at her expectantly, his eyes slightly slumbrous, slightly teasing. Then he reached for her hand, capturing it in one of his. 'Fine, we'll talk soberly.' He grinned at the pun. 'So, what's the problem?'

Samantha tried to tug her hand away, to keep her dignity, but Jason held fast, and unless she wanted to turn this into a wrestling match, she'd have to let him. 'The problem is Toby,' she managed after a moment. 'Andrea is infatuated with him. And——' she groped for a good way to put it '—the feeling seems to be mutual.'

One eyebrow cocked. 'So?'

She stared at him, indignant. 'So? *So?* He's almost twenty years old. She's a child!'

'She's a young woman.'

'You mean you don't care?'

Jason lifted his shoulders. 'Well, I mean, what did he do to her?'

'He...he kissed her.'

Jason's jaw went slack. 'He...kissed her?' His eyes widened. He started to laugh. 'Is that all? Is that what you're fluttering about? A single kiss?'

'I am *not* fluttering,' Samantha retorted. 'I am being paid to chaperon your sister. I presumed that meant that you wanted her "chaperoned".'

'It meant I wanted someone to be her companion, her friend, and to give her a bit of womanly *twentieth century* advice.' Jason shook his head. 'It meant I wanted someone to warn the leches off. But...Toby?' He began to laugh again.

'You don't perceive Toby as a threat, then, I take it?' Samantha said stiffly.

'I don't perceive Toby as a threat,' Jason said with as much solemnity as he could muster. But it didn't stop a corner of his mouth from twitching into a grin.

'Very well.' Samantha yanked her hand out of his and got to her feet.

Jason came to his and stood, looming, dark and male, scant inches from her. 'You see kisses as threats, Samantha?' he asked softly.

He wasn't touching her, but she felt as if he were. She could see the shallow rise and fall of his chest, could feel the warmth of his breath. She swallowed and stepped back, turning to go to her bedroom. His hand on her arm halted her.

'Sam?'

She tried to shake him off, but his grip held her fast.

'I asked you a question. Do you?' he persisted.

'Not . . . necessarily.'

He touched her chin, lifting her face so that she was forced to either look at him or close her eyes. 'When I kissed you, was I threatening you?'

'Jason, please . . .'

'I didn't mean to threaten you, Samantha.' His voice was whisper-soft, his thumb stroked her cheek, his dark blue eyes delved into hers.

And even as she watched, mesmerised, his face came down towards hers, his nose brushed against her nose, and then his lips met hers. It was the opposite of a threat. It was gentle, seeking, tentative. And then, abruptly, just when Samantha's breathing quickened and her response grew, it was gone.

'Kisses should never be threats, Samantha,' Jason said softly. 'A kiss should always be a promise.'

Samantha didn't sleep a wink all night. Her mind churned with visions of Jason's face, dark and unreadable, yet strangely tender. It grappled with the remembered taste of his lips. It swam with earlier, harsher memories of other lips, of other faces. First Fritz's, hungry and demanding, then Oliver's, sweet and undemanding, as unresponsive as her own at their mutual touch.

Neither was remotely like Jason's. Neither evoked remotely the response that Jason's did. She tossed this way and that, threw off the covers, retrieved them and tucked them around her again.

'Composure is vital,' her father always said.

Composure was impossible, thought Samantha. She couldn't handle this. Whatever she had once thought about being able to stick it out here for the summer, she was wrong. There was no way on earth she would be able to live in equanimity with Jason Cole. He unnerved her, undermined her, undid her strongest resolve. And he thought she was a fool as well.

How he'd laughed when she'd said that Toby had kissed Andrea! How Victorian he'd thought her outrage! How right he was.

It might be different, she acknowledged, if the kisses Jason had given her had meant something to him. They didn't. If he was really interested in anyone, it was Dena McGarvey. He'd just spent until two a.m. proving it. Samantha was no more than a toy to him, someone to be dallied with, teased, harassed and, if luck was with him, to spend the night with. But no more than that.

It would be more than that to her.

Samantha touched her lips. They tingled even now. They taunted her, wanting more. And more of Jason

Cole was out of the question. It was simply a matter of self-preservation.

She would go on the road trip to Florida, since it would be too late to hire someone else. But after they got back, she was through. She would break her contract. Let him take her to court.

Her father would defend her. He would be only too happy to hire her a lawyer once he knew what sort of man Jason Cole was. And he would be delighted to know that she'd given up this teaching nonsense and had come to her senses at last. He'd probably even find her a nice talented musician to nurture if Oliver didn't come up to scratch.

Resolution made, she got up and showered, then dressed once more in the frumpy skirt and blouse combo that she knew Jason despised. It was armour, and she admitted it. But she knew she had learned her limits, and she knew she needed all the defences she could get.

Then she went in search of Jason, committed to telling him at once. She found him in the living-room on the phone. He was frowning as he scribbled something on a piece of paper.

'Who? Spell that.' Then, 'Never heard of him.'

He spotted Samantha and beckoned to her urgently. 'Tell it to Ms Peabody,' he instructed the caller. 'She'll know.' Before Samantha could object, he thrust the phone into her hand.

'Ah, Ms Peabody,' came a familiar boom. 'Hortense Strong here.'

Samantha swallowed a groan. 'Uh—yes, Mrs Strong. What can I do for you?'

'*You* know who Raul Ibañez is, I trust?'

'Of course.' One of the world's premier cellists, and a friend of her father, the one he often wanted her to play for, the one Samantha had always refused to play for because she knew she didn't have the talent.

'Well, he's going to hear Andrea.'

'*What?*'

'I thought you'd be delighted.' Hortense was practically beaming óver the telephone line. 'Know him well, I do. Went to school with his wife, Letty. Years ago that was, of course. But I got to·thinking, no reason why Raul shouldn't hear her if she's as good as you say.'

Oh, lord. 'I don't think——'

'You don't think she's good enough?' Hortense barked.

'Er—well, no, I didn't say that. I——' Marshalling her thoughts, Samantha realised that Andrea indeed might possibly be good enough. 'I'm just surprised,' Samantha stammered finally. 'She's excellent, of course. I just never considered...'

'Well, I did. Called him last night and asked him. Told him about Andrea. Said she was doing well, had a good teacher. Wanted him to hear her.'

'And he said yes?'

'Of course.' Hortense didn't seem to think there was ever any doubt.

Samantha knew how wrong that was. Raul Ibañez did not listen to teenage cellists as a matter of course. He was an impatient old codger who sometimes made her father look like the personification of sweetness and light. It was a miracle as well as a great honour that he'd consented.

'Told him you were making a world of difference,' Hortense went on. 'Jason says so.'

'*Jason* says so?' Samantha shot him a furious glance and swallowed hard. What on earth did Jason know about it? Volleyball, yes; cellos, hardly.

'Did you tell him...who her teacher was?' If Raul knew it was Samantha and said so, there was no way Hortense would go on thinking she was close to fifty.

'Couldn't remember your first name. All I knew was the Peabody part,' Hortense replied. 'He wanted to know if you were related to Ambrose Peabody. Are you?'

'Remotely,' Samantha allowed. Though why she should be concerned with protecting Jason's interests at this point she couldn't imagine.

'Thought so,' Hortense said briskly. 'Talent runs in families. Well, I hope the Peabody skill is enough to make Raul sit up and take notice. He'll hear her in the Hamptons in August.'

'The Hamptons?' Samantha echoed.

'Happy coincidence,' Hortense said. 'You'll be there with Jason at the same time that the music festival takes place.'

'But Mrs——'

'Must fly,' Hortense said briskly. 'Just you make sure Andrea does well. Don't want Raul to think his time is wasted. Might take her as a student, he says. Ta ta.'

She rang off, leaving Samantha staring at the receiver in her hand. Gently Jason took it away from her and set it down. Samantha stared at him, dumbfounded.

'Your aunt's got Raul Ibañez listening to Andrea.'

'That's good?'

'That's amazing.' She still couldn't quite believe it.

'Well, you wanted Andi to have a challenge.'

Samantha shook her head. 'Yes, but—Raul Ibañez?'

'Big gun, huh?'

'You could say that,' Samantha murmured. Raul Ibañez. How she would love to have Andrea do well, impress Raul, justify her summer. Except she wasn't staying.

'Well, then, we'll have to be sure she pulls it off,' Jason went on.

'I—no!'

'No? What's the matter?' He was pouring her a glass of orange juice and setting a plate of pancakes in front of her as he spoke.

'I can't—I don't——' But Samantha's resolution was wavering. She'd never wanted to play for Raul Ibañez herself, but to have a student like Andrea play was a powerful temptation. It would be a great justification for her teaching career.

The teaching career she was giving up, she reminded herself. The teaching career she would have no time for once she married Oliver.

But still . . . the very idea of Raul Ibañez being willing to hear Andrea. And if he were to accept Andrea as a student! Surely her father and Oliver couldn't sneeze at that. Surely that would be a *coup*, a success, something that would make her father proud. But at what cost . . . ?

Her mind went back to the night before, to the touch of Jason's lips, to his 'promise'. There was no question but that he meant every word. Did she dare risk it?

'Don't worry so much. She'll be able to do it,' Jason was saying. He stood with his palms pressing flat on the table, his blue eyes confident as he looked down at her. 'Coles always rise to the challenge.'

Samantha looked at him warily. That was exactly what she was afraid of.

But Jason was smiling at her, looking earnest and confident and not at all like the man who had kissed her with such tenderness last night. No, that wasn't quite right, Samantha thought. He was still that man, but there was another side to him here.

'I'll even see that Toby doesn't bother her,' he went on.

Samantha blinked.

'I mean it.'

But that, Samantha could have told him, was only half the problem. If she was going to stay, she needed Jason to promise that *he* would stop bothering *her*.

'Honestly, Sam, you've got plenty of time to get her ready,' Jason went on, taking her silence for indecision based on Andrea's competence. He chewed his pancakes reflectively. 'We don't play in the Hamptons until mid-August.'

Samantha didn't answer; she was still trying to come to grips with Raul Ibañez, with not leaving.

'Sam?'

She mustered a glare.

'Sorry,' he said quickly. 'Samantha, I mean.' He gave her another earnest look, worried and endearing. 'You *can* do it, can't you?' he asked, hesitant for the first time.

Of course she *could*. At least, she hoped so. And Andrea could, too, if she was willing to work. But doing so meant really concentrating, avoiding distractions, staying clear of Toby Henning. And, for Samantha, it meant staying clear of Jason Cole.

The phone rang again. Jason picked it up. His expression changed, lightening almost at once. 'Dena! How're you doing this morning, sweetheart?'

Samantha steeled her heart, her mind, her emotions. She could do it, she told herself. She could teach Andrea, she could impress Raul Ibañez, she could make a name for herself as a top-notch teacher.

She *would* do it. And, in doing so, she would prove once and for all that she had her priorities straight. She would prove herself a teacher that her father could be proud of. And she would prove to herself that she could resist Jason Cole.

It would be easy enough, she told herself, once they got on the road. With a tournament to occupy his mind, Jason wouldn't have time to bother her.

At least, that was what she thought until that evening when they landed in Tampa, then drove to the tournament site down the Florida Gulf coast, and Jason carried their suitcases into a hotel suite.

Depositing the cases on the floor, he dropped down on to the sofa beside it. 'Thank heaven for air-conditioning,' he sighed, and began to unbutton his shirt.

'Do you mind?' Samantha said sharply.

Jason blinked. 'Huh?'

'Do you think you could wait until you get to your own room to undress?'

There was a pause. 'My own room?'

Samantha opened her mouth, then closed it again. Surely he didn't think...surely he didn't intend... 'Jason,' she began in a low, warning tone.

'Samantha,' he said in mocking mimicry.

'You're not...'

'It's a suite, for cripes' sake.' He stood up, threw off his shirt and spread his arms. '*Two* rooms, Samantha. Behold—a bedroom right through there for you and Andrea. A living-room with sofa bed here for Toby and me.'

'*Toby?*' It was more a yelp than a question.

'You call me?' Toby appeared in the doorway, innocent and unaware, his duffel bag and Andrea's in his hands.

'No. Never mind,' Samantha muttered. She nailed Jason with another glare and jerked her head towards the bedroom. 'I need to talk to you.'

Jason shrugged. He followed her meekly into the bedroom and dropped down on to the bed, stretching out and folding his hands behind his head. Samantha glowered at him, but didn't speak until she had shut the door. Then she rounded on him and folded her arms across her breasts. 'This isn't going to work.'

'What isn't?' Jason dredged up an innocent look of his own.

'This "suite" business.'

'It has to.'

'Why? Surely you can afford two rooms.'

'Of course I can afford two rooms. But Hortense won't allow it.'

Samantha gaped. '*Hortense* won't allow it?'

Jason nodded. 'You don't like the set-up, blame her.'

'Why?'

'Because she's threatened to pop up at any moment.' His mouth twisted derisively. 'To see that Andrea is "being supervised".'

'I'll be supervising.'

'Yeah, but we aren't desperate for her to meet you, are we? And anyway, if she finds out I'm not actively being Andrea's guardian, you can bet she'll make something of it. If I've got my own room, she'll think I have women in it all night. Whereas if I'm stuck in a suite with old battleaxe Peabody——' he grinned at her '—she knows I won't.'

'Very funny.'

Jason smiled and stretched his arms over his head. Samantha found her eyes riveted to his stomach muscles. 'I thought you'd appreciate the irony.'

Samantha grimaced and looked away.

'I won't bite, sweetheart. Not here at least,' he added with a wink.

Samantha took a step backwards. Jason sat up swiftly, reached out and caught her hand, then touched her chin with his fingers. He drew her face down, then brought his lips to touch hers lightly. 'Relax, Sam,' he counselled. 'Relax and enjoy.'

But Samantha didn't dare. If she let down her guard for an instant, who knew what would become of her?

It was hard, however, to keep up her shield when all around her were merrily having a good time. Most of the other players were staying at the same hotel, and, while they might be fierce opponents on the court, she had learned that they were laughing, teasing compatriots off it.

She hadn't seen too much of them while they were at home, preferring to keep her distance. But at the hotel it was more difficult. And it didn't take Samantha long to realise why Jason didn't consider Toby a threat to Andrea. It was all a matter of degree. And Toby Henning was a veritable pussy-cat compared to several of the more intrepid Casanovas Jason introduced her to in the lobby as they went out to eat at a nearby restaurant.

'I begin to understand the reason for a chaperon,' Samantha said.

'Good,' Jason replied grimly. 'Stay away from them.'

'With pleasure.' For once she didn't resent his imperious tone.

After eating, Jason excused himself. He was more than simply a player here. He was involved not only in the tournament, but also in the set-up and in the organisation of the booth selling NetWork clothing. He had a thousand small details to deal with, people to see, places to check out, and he commandeered Toby to help him.

'You'll be all right?' he asked Samantha.

'Of course,' she assured him. 'If we're not, I'm not earning my keep.'

'If you're not, we're in big trouble,' Jason said flatly.

'Don't worry,' Samantha promised as he and Toby left. 'We'll be fine. We can watch TV in the room.'

'Watch TV?' Andrea was aghast. 'But this is Florida! I've never been to Florida before. Let's just go out and walk around,' she pleaded. 'And later, Toby said there was this party and——'

'No parties.' Samantha was adamant.

Andrea looked as if she might protest, but then she only sighed. 'A walk, then?'

Samantha supposed she could agree to that much. She'd never been to Florida either. Besides, they couldn't exactly come to grief in the middle of a busy Florida street, even if accosted by a dozen Casanovas. 'All right.'

They wandered along the boulevard, looking in the windows of boutiques and bikini shops, reading the advertisements for Disney World, Boardwalk and baseball, and numerous jai alai frontons. They walked far enough to feel hungry again, so they bought ice-cream dipped in milk chocolate and coated with rainbow sprinkles at

Häagen Daz, and decided that standard brands made both coasts remarkably similar.

Samantha thought this wasn't going to be too difficult after all. Because it was early, she even agreed to playing a game of miniature golf at an amusement area before they headed towards the hotel.

They were just starting back when two very tall blond men with devastating white grins and dark tans loomed in front of them. Samantha ignored them.

'Well, hello again. Fancy meeting you here.' The better-looking of the two gave Samantha a hungry once-over. His hair flopped in his eyes and he shoved it back. 'Sammie, isn't it?'

'Samantha.' She didn't remember his name, only his face. He was one of the two-bit Casanovas Jason had warned her away from. She gave him a brief nod and moved purposefully on.

He fell into step beside her. The other joined Andrea, removing her from Samantha like a cowboy cutting out a heifer.

'Jason says you're a musician,' Flop Hair went on, undeterred, matching his steps to hers.

'Yes.' Samantha kept right on walking. Hard, warm fingers suddenly laced with hers and she stopped stock-still.

Flop Hair spun her around so she was face to face with him. 'I bet we could make beautiful music, honey,' he drawled.

Samantha jerked away. 'Not at all. I think it would be cacophonous in the extreme. Come along, Andrea,' she snapped.

'Andi wants to go to the party, don't you, Andi?' said the other one.

'Of course, I——'

'No parties,' Samantha said, feeling like a dragon.

'But——'

'No!'

'How 'bout a swim, then?' Flop Hair suggested.

'No, thank you.'

'A beer?'

'Please, Mr—er...'

'Then how 'bout a quickie?' Flop Hair breathed right in Samantha's ear.

Her face flamed. She shot a quick glance at Andrea, but the other girl seemed merely bemused and not nearly as flustered as Samantha herself.

'No, thank you,' she said with icy precision. 'Good evening.' And she snatched Andrea away, practically dragging the girl behind her.

'Hey, don't forget the party. Hutch's room. Y'all come!' he called after her, determined to the last. 'See you there.'

Not, Samantha thought grimly, if I see you first.

Andrea still wanted to go to the party. 'Why not?' she demanded when they got back to the room. 'Toby will be there.'

'Toby isn't fifteen.'

'Neither are you.'

'I'm not going either.' Samantha wouldn't have gone no matter what age she was. Loud, raucous parties were not her style. The very thought made her shudder.

Andrea flung herself into the chair and glowered. 'What if Toby meets another girl?'

Samantha rather wished he would. Maybe it would take some of the hunger out of his gaze whenever he looked at Andrea. But she didn't want to hurt Andrea's feelings by saying so. She wasn't sure exactly why she knew it would hurt Andrea so much, but haunting memories of her own feelings when she thought of Jason with Dena McGarvey might have had something to do with it.

'You're worth any girl he's likely to meet,' she said placatingly.

Andrea still grumbled. But, when Samantha couldn't be moved, she went off complaining to take a long hot shower, then settled in bed to read. 'A Nancy Drew mystery,' she fumed, waving the book in Samantha's direction. 'All the excitement I'll ever get in my life.'

Samantha shrugged. 'Enjoy.' She shut herself in the living-room with a magazine. But before long the noise from the party filtered through the walls. Wherever Hutch's was, it wasn't far.

The beat of the music made her restless. The echo of laughter taunted her as well. Was Jason there, too? She found herself listening to see if she could catch the sound of his voice; then she berated herself: why did she care?

She didn't. She buried herself again in the magazine, then, when that didn't distract her, turned on the television. Shortly after eleven, when the noise-level reached the point where she couldn't even feign interest in the Friday night film any more, she got up and went into the bedroom.

Andrea was sound asleep, the light on, the book lying open at her side. It really was a new, updated Nancy Drew book. Samantha smiled. What an amazing collection of contradictory impulses and enthusiasms made up Andrea Cole. Eager woman of the world one moment, child at heart the next. And a tremendously talented musician along with it all.

The girl was a far more complicated package than Samantha could have imagined when she'd agreed to be Andrea's teacher-chaperon just scant weeks ago. Why had she ever thought that spending the summer this way would—Jason aside—be a piece of cake?

Because when Andrea had been little more than her student at Rudley, the musician side of her was almost all of her Samantha saw. And now? Now she saw in Andrea a decided resemblance to her older brother. It was there in the determined lower lip, in the strong chin, in the line of the jaw. Softened, perhaps, but still evident.

It was there in the personality, too. In their own ways, both Coles were stubborn, determined, hard workers. The trouble was, now Andrea seemed to want to play as hard as Jason did, too. And she couldn't. Samantha wasn't supposed to let her.

She sighed, wondering if Jason had any idea how difficult that was going to be.

She changed into her nightgown and shut off the light, then slipped between the sheets. The noise was less, but she still couldn't sleep. The bass throbbed on, and, over the hum of the air-conditioning, the shouts and laughs of the party-goers were still all too clear.

Andrea had been certain Toby would be there. Was Jason? Undoubtedly. Where else would he be on a night like tonight?

Samantha sighed, flopping this way and that. But there was no dozing, no gradual drifting off to sleep. Finally she got back up, pulled on her dressing-gown and padded back out to the living-room. She flipped on the television and scanned the channels, but nothing appealed. She stared out the window, then picked up the book that Jason had tossed on the table next to the sofa. It was a mystery. Not the spine-tingling thriller type, but a more thoughtful cultural sort that took place in the southwest, mostly on the Navajo reservation. Never having been there, Samantha was entranced. Once she began reading, the party faded and she couldn't put the book down.

It was a surprise when, quite some time later, the door opened and she looked up to see Jason. If she was disconcerted to see him, he looked equally surprised to see her. His eyes widened slightly and he halted for a moment. Samantha steeled herself for the requisite smart remark, but it was not forthcoming.

Instead Jason just kneaded the back of his neck wearily and gave her a rueful grin. 'Still up?'

'Couldn't sleep,' Samantha replied cautiously. Her gaze drifted towards the general direction of the noise.

Had he just come from there? It didn't look like it. He looked as though he'd come from a war. Her inclination to flee melted away in the face of his weariness.

Even as she studied him, he crossed the room and sank down on to the sofa beside her, stretching out his long legs and dropping his head against the back. He shut his eyes and let out a long breath. 'Lord, what a night.'

'Bad?'

His eyes opened and he turned his head so that his eyes met hers. 'Awful is more like it.'

'What happened?'

Jason sighed. 'What didn't?' He pressed the heels of his hands against his eyes and rubbed them, then raked his fingers through his hair, kneading his scalp as if he'd just taken off a hat several sizes too small.

Samantha's fingers knotted, clutching the book tightly to keep from reaching for his tense shoulders. Instinctively she wanted to soothe the frustration she saw in him, the weariness, the exhaustion. She practically had to sit on her hands not to do so.

'It started out with a permit problem,' Jason said. 'I went down to see how the set-up was going, and some city guy was there saying we needed to file a different permit to use the beach for commercial purposes. I said we'd filed the permit. He didn't have a record of it. Three hours of bureaucratic hassle was spent clearing that up.

'Then some of the gear didn't arrive. I had to call LA about a hundred times to track it down. The truck had broken down. So then I had to find alternative gear. By the time I rounded it up, it was, naturally, too late for commercial delivery, so I had to rent a truck and move it myself...' He gave her a weak grin. 'I was going to jog tonight. Ha—I never did get it in. Or anything else, for that matter...'

'Like the...party?'

'Party?'

'Someone said——' she paused awkwardly '——Hutch's.' In her silence the music and the shrill feminine laughter made her explanations for her.

Jason grimaced. 'I never go to those.'

'You don't?'

'How the hell can you win a volleyball tournament if you're hungover?'

'I guess...you can't,' she said weakly.

'Damned right you can't. Most of us try to get an early night. The ones who are serious, anyway. Why would I fly clear across the country and then party myself into extinction? I wouldn't have a chance tomorrow.'

'Andrea said Toby was going.'

'Young fool. Hope to hell he gets home before he gets plastered. If not, I'll have to go rout him out.'

'Yes.' But whether Toby got plastered or not, Samantha felt, for some odd reason, immeasurably lighter. She smiled at Jason.

Jason smiled back.

Seconds ticked past. Minutes. The smiles moved beyond their mouths to their eyes, and then their whole faces. And then smiles weren't enough. Their expressions began to warm, to beckon, to need.

Slowly and with great deliberation, Jason reached for Samantha, slid his arms around her and drew her close to him, fitting her body to his.

She should resist, Samantha told herself. She *had* to resist, to pull back, reject him, protect herself. But nothing in her wanted to do it. She had been holding back, protecting herself for so long.

'Don't be afraid,' Jason whispered as if he read her thoughts, and mindlessly, obediently, Samantha whispered back,

'No. I'm not.'

And the oddest thing was, it was true.

For once Jason didn't seem threatening to her. He didn't mock or tease or intimidate. He simply needed;

and Samantha, fists slowly uncurling, met that need with one of her own.

His lips touched hers gently, seeking, not demanding, and she remembered his words about kisses and promises. This kiss felt like a promise, a promise that Samantha wanted desperately for him to keep. Her lips parted slightly, softening for him, and she felt him smile.

'Ah, Sam,' he murmured. 'My Sam.'

This time she didn't object to the nickname. Instead she kissed him back. Tentatively, tremulously, her hands crept up and touched his upper arms, then slid around his back, holding him closer.

It was an amazing feeling, this warm, strong, vital body responding to hers. So different. New. A feeling she'd never felt before. Not with Fritz. Not with Oliver.

One of Jason's hands touched her hair, smoothed it back away from her face, then traced the line of her jaw, the shell of her ear, the curve of her neck. His hands were rough and callused, volleyball player's hands. And, wherever he touched, Samantha's nerve-endings sang, her body vibrated with the same intensity that her cello did under the vibrato of her fingers.

Jason's breathing quickened. He urged her on to his lap, cuddling her close, making her aware of his arousal. But for once Samantha didn't find that threatening either. There was nothing aggressive in his touch. He was asking, not insisting. He never demanded. He made no attempt to push her further.

And, because he didn't, she wanted to go further herself. She wanted to assuage that need in him, to assuage the need he was creating in her.

Her hands slid around to touch his chest. They stroked downwards across the soft cotton of his T-shirt and brushed the waistband of his jeans. Jason sucked in his breath, his hips surged, his lips pressed hungrily against her neck.

Emboldened at his response, Samantha let her hands sink an inch further. She felt Jason's heart pound wildly, his breathing grow laboured. Her own heart was stampeding, her breathing gone wild.

He needed... She needed...

And then there came a thump, a key rattled in the door, and Toby stumbled into the room.

Samantha practically flew to the other end of the couch, patting her hair, straightening her dressing-gown, gasping for breath.

'Cripes,' Jason muttered, sucking air.

Toby looked around and gave them a slightly sloshed grin. 'How ya doin'?' He wandered further into the room, blinked, then pushed his blond hair back out of his eyes. 'Don' mind me,' he told them with a credible wink. 'I know what you're doin'. Go right ahead. Do it m'self if I weren't too——' He shook his head and groaned, 'Hell, m'head. Feels like 'n'elephant's sittin' on it.'

'One should be,' Jason muttered under his breath as he got up and grabbed Toby by the arm, hauling him unceremoniously towards the bathroom.

The look he gave Samantha was both rueful and regretful. 'Sorry about this.'

Then the door closed behind them, and Samantha heard the water to the shower begin to run. There were a few bumps and groans, then Toby let out a 'Lord almighty! That's cold!' and Jason said implacably,

'Tough. Wake up and face reality, chum.'

Samantha, still shuddering in the corner of the sofa, took the advice to heart.

What on earth had possessed her? How could she have kissed him that way? Her cheeks burned at the memory. She could still feel the hardness of his body against hers, the taste of his skin, the harshness of his breathing.

She tried to forget it. She couldn't. Her body was still quivering for him, still aching to be touched, to be caressed, and her mind wouldn't shield her from it.

Idiot, she accused herself, getting to her feet, commanding her legs to hold her as she crossed the room quickly and shut herself in the bedroom with the peacefully sleeping Andrea. Once there she leaned against the door, barricading it as if all the devils in hell were after her.

How could you let him come on to you that way? *Let him?* she asked herself. She'd encouraged him!

Now she was angry. Angry at Jason. Angry at herself. She knew the way he teased her, the way he was constantly trying to undermine her resolve. He'd told her to loosen up, to relax, to have a good time just today. And over the past few weeks he'd certainly offered to show her how often enough.

Tonight he must have thought he'd had a chance to prove to her exactly what he meant!

The water stopped in the bathroom and she could hear Jason's gruff voice lecturing Toby about something. It didn't take much imagination to guess what. Toby was probably getting very strict instructions about not barging into hotel rooms where his mentor was entertaining women. Toby seemed to be saying, 'uh-huh' a lot. It figured.

Samantha bit her lip, humiliated. How could she have been such a fool? Well, she wasn't going to be. Not ever again.

She heard the door open to the bathroom. Footsteps went back into the living-room, then approached the door to the bedroom.

'Samantha?'

She didn't answer.

The knob rattled. Please, no, she begged silently, glad she'd locked the door.

His voice came again, low and persistent. 'Sam? Sam! Open up.'

'Go away.'

'Look, I'm sorry it happened this way.'

'I'm glad,' she said fiercely.

There was a pause. Then, 'What? Why?' His whisper was outraged.

'I must have been insane!' she said bitterly.

'Bull. You wanted——'

'Never mind what I did or didn't want. I *don't* want it now, so leave me alone,' she hissed through the closed door.

'Come on, Sam!'

'And stop calling me Sam!'

Before he could say anything else she walked away from the door, crossed the room and slid between the sheets of her bed. Andrea sighed, rolled over, and went on sleeping. Samantha envied her the ability.

She lay flat on her back and listened to Jason's urgent whispering, Toby's banging and thumping, and knew it was going to be a very long night.

CHAPTER SEVEN

BUT, unfortunately, not long enough. Shortly after four in the morning, Samantha heard a faint rattle, then a click, and the bedroom door eased open. Samantha froze. The heavy curtains left the room in enough darkness so she couldn't make the intruder out clearly, but there was no doubt who it was.

Her eyes snapped shut, and she concentrated on breathing naturally, sighing easily, rolling over as if she were in the midst of deepest sleep.

'Cut it out, Sam. I know you're awake.'

She didn't move.

'I thought you might come to your senses and come out and talk to me,' he went on conversationally, 'but since you didn't...' She could tell he shrugged. He jiggled her toe.

Samantha rolled back over and scowled up at him. 'How'd you get in here? I locked the door.'

Jason gave her an unrepentant smile. 'I'm a man of many talents. And I have a credit card.'

'I thought they only did that in movies.'

'Think again.' His smile made Samantha shiver.

'What do you want?'

'To talk.'

'I don't want to talk.'

A grin flickered across his face. 'Well, I can think of other things I'd rather do, too, but——'

'Stop it,' she hissed, stiffening.

He sank down on the bed next to her. Samantha wriggled away as far as she could so that they weren't touching.

116

'You weren't averse to "other things" last night,' Jason reminded her.

'I was a fool last night,' she said bitterly.

'No, you weren't. Not then. Now's a different story.'

In the other bed, Andrea muttered and rolled over. Samantha glared at Jason. 'Get out of here. What's Andrea going to think if she wakes up?'

'If you're worried, come with me.'

'Come with you?' Samantha looked at him as if he'd lost his mind.

'For a walk. Just a walk. We need to talk,' he repeated.

Why? Nothing was going to change. He wasn't going to declare undying love. And if he did, he wouldn't mean it and she wouldn't want him. But she couldn't see another way of getting rid of him. And having Andrea wake up to find him on her bed was more than she could bear.

'All right,' Samantha muttered. 'Get out and let me get dressed.'

Jason considered that. 'Ten minutes and I'm coming in after you.'

'Just go,' she bit out. She waited until he had shut the door behind him before she got out of bed.

She had twenty-seven seconds left, by her reckoning, when she opened the door. Jason was standing on the other side, his eyes on his watch. When she appeared he gave her a tight smile, then nodded his head towards the door and turned on his heel. Obedient as a pet poodle, Samantha thought irritably, she followed him.

Jason didn't say anything until they were heading across the car park towards the road that bordered the beach. Then he slowed his pace and turned to her. 'I'm sorry about Toby last night.'

'I'm not,' Samantha said shortly.

A muscle ticked in Jason's jaw. 'You seem to think he saved you from a fate worse than death.'

'You could say that.'

His hand snaked out and grabbed hers, hauling her to a stop at the edge of the pavement that led down to the beach. 'Why?'

Samantha couldn't believe he had to ask. She just stared at him. 'Think about it.'

He was either a terrific actor or he was stupid, because he continued to look totally baffled. 'Look,' he said at last, 'Maybe I moved too fast for you. Maybe I——'

'Fast doesn't even come into it. You shouldn't be moving on me at all. I'm your employee.'

'Sexual harassment?' He gave her a mocking look. 'Is that what you're claiming, Sam?'

She clenched her teeth, but he went right on, 'I don't think so. Not with the response you gave me. I might have kissed you, Samantha Peabody. But you sure as hell were kissing me back!'

She tried to jerk away from him, but he hung on grimly. 'Let go!'

'No way.' Jason tugged her down the steps and on to the beach, and there, in the rosy dawn, he kissed her again. Not merely kissed her, knocked her right off her feet. His mouth was firm and persuasive, the teasing gone, the asking gone. This time he was demanding.

Samantha closed her lips and tried to spurn him. Without success. The kiss went on. And on. And the longer it lasted, the harder it became to resist, the more Samantha wanted to share in it, the more she couldn't *help* but respond to it.

Unwillingly at first, then desperately, her arms crept up around his neck, holding him closer as her mouth met his with a fury and a need that matched his own. Their bodies touched from knee to nose, their hearts pounded in unison. And, when at last they had to breathe, it seemed to Samantha that they did so with one breath.

Jason rested his forehead against hers as he tried to regain control. After a moment, he took a deep, shuddering breath. 'I...told you so,' he said softly and one corner of his mouth lifted in a quirky grin.

It was the way he said it that did her in. Not gruff, not superior. Rueful, almost. Gentle. As if he was simply acknowledging the inevitable. And all Samantha could do was acknowledge it, too. She didn't have to like it, didn't even have to want it. But she couldn't deny it, either.

'What...what about Dena?' she stammered finally.

He frowned. 'What about her?'

'She...you...you and she are...'

'Friends,' Jason said firmly.

'Friends?' Samantha couldn't help the scepticism in her voice. There was a bond between Dena and Jason. A link stronger than simple friendship.

'Forget Dena. Dena has nothing to do with you and me.' Jason's voice was flat. He reached for her hand. 'She's not important. Believe me. Come on.'

Confused, Samantha allowed herself to be towed towards the water. The fiery sunrise turned Jason's hair bronze and gave him a warrior's fierceness as he squinted into it. But his hold on Samantha's hand was gentle, and the look he gave her when he turned his gaze to meet hers was warm.

He could have gloated. He could have been rude and overbearing and been perfectly within his rights. But he wasn't. She didn't know what to expect now, but she knew she didn't expect what she got, which was simply a long walk on the beach in companionable silence.

'Don't trust men like him,' her father had told her after he'd rescued her from the folly of Fritz. 'They only want one thing. They'll use you and throw you away.'

But Jason wasn't using. He wasn't throwing. He was treating her with a gentleness she'd never found in another man. Was it possible, she wondered, that about this one man her father could be wrong?

Her mind still buzzed with questions about Dena, about Jason's relationship with her, about why she didn't matter. But she couldn't find the words to ask, couldn't have asked even if she had found the words because she sensed a wall there. Whatever existed between Jason and Dena was something he wasn't going to talk about.

But for now she found that she trusted his assurance, and so she simply walked with him, bemused, amazed, and surprisingly glad to be there, glad to have his hand wrapped around hers.

It was past six by the time they turned back. Early morning joggers and dog-walkers were out and about, and surfers were trying, though rarely succeeding, to find a wave worth riding to shore. She and Jason stood on the beach watching them for a while.

'I'm famished,' he said finally. 'You must be, too.' And when she admitted she was he led her into a beachy, palm-tree-and-pineapple sort of place advertising coconut-milk pancakes and sourdough French toast.

They ordered, the waitress brought them coffee, and only then, surrounded by several other couples staring into each other's starry eyes, did Samantha begin to feel awkward.

'Don't,' Jason said abruptly.

'Don't what?'

'Stare at your lap and tear your napkin to shreds. Nothing's going to happen that you don't want to happen.'

Samantha looked across the table at him. 'I'm not sure what I want to happen,' she said with an honesty that surprised even herself.

Jason smiled. 'Well, that's progress at least.'

Samantha wasn't sure. But their pancakes arrived then, and the aroma was so enticing that she stopped fretting for a few moments and allowed herself to savour her meal.

Jason seemed similarly inclined. He dug right in and didn't surface again until his plate was clean and he was sipping his third cup of coffee. Then he regarded Samantha solemnly over the rim of the cup and said, 'You'll come and watch today, won't you?'

'The games, you mean?'

'Me, I mean.'

She swallowed, her fingers tightening around the handle of her cup. 'I should think you'd want fans there. Up front. Cheering you on. People who know what's going on.'

'I want *you*.'

Samantha felt an icy current run right down the length of her spine at the same time that his gaze was burning her.

'Will you come?' His voice was soft.

'Another one of my "duties"?' she said, trying for a lightness she didn't really feel.

Jason frowned. 'Is that the way you want to see it?'

'I——' It wasn't. Not really. But, as she'd told him, she didn't know what she did want. She swallowed. 'I'll come.'

Jason took her hand in his and gave it a gentle squeeze. 'Good.'

Andrea was just getting up when they returned, and if she thought it strange to find them coming in, breakfast already over at seven in the morning, she didn't say. She seemed far more interested in Toby, who was still dead to the world on the convertible sofa.

'Wake him up,' Jason said gruffly.

'But he needs his sleep,' Andrea protested.

Jason gave her a baleful look. 'If he'd needed his sleep he could have got home earlier.'

Andrea's face fell. 'You mean he was...'

'I mean, he's slept long enough. I've got a hundred last-minute details to see to. And I want you to see that he gets to the court on time, do you understand? I'm counting on you. He's your responsibility.'

Jason couldn't have said anything more inclined to bring his little sister into line. Andrea beamed. 'He'll be there.'

Jason fixed Samantha with a level stare. 'And I'm counting on you to take care of them both.'

Samantha smiled. 'Who's going to take care of me?'

Jason smiled back. 'I'll take care of you, sweetheart. It will be my greatest pleasure.'

Andrea looked up, startled. 'Oh, wow,' she breathed, Toby momentarily forgotten. Samantha went absolutely scarlet. Jason winked and vanished out the door.

They got Toby to the court on time. Barely. He was not an early morning person. He kept rolling over and burying his head under the pillow, and, when they finally got him up, he held his head in his hands, grumbling. Andrea was inclined to baby him along, but Samantha wasn't sympathetic in the least.

'I was up as late as you were,' she told him flatly as she herded him out the door.

Toby looked at her for a long moment. Then, 'I'll say you were,' he replied, and he gave her a wide grin and a blatant wink that made her toes curl.

When they arrived at the beach, Toby pointed to the players' tent where several men not playing were chatting easily and fooling around. 'Jason's over there.'

He was not fooling around at all, but was engaged in earnest conversation with a man in, of all things, a suit and tie. He didn't even notice their approach. Samantha would happily not have approached at all. But Toby was insistent.

'Gotta get you two right up front.'

'Oh, but——'

Jason's gaze swivelled away from the man when he heard her brief protest. He gave her a heart-stopping grin. 'You made it.'

'Of course we made it,' Toby said testily.

'Mmm.' Jason scarcely spared him a glance. His eyes were all for Samantha. 'I'll get back to you,' he told the man in the suit. He held out his hand to Samantha and when, hesitantly, she took it, he drew her forward and planted a kiss smack on her lips.

'Didn't think I'd dreamed it,' Toby said with a grin.

'Oh, wow,' Andrea murmured again.

Samantha shot her an irritable glance and tried to draw her hand away from Jason's, but he led her towards the main court where a game was in progress.

A friend had saved them places, he told her, nodding his head towards the front row of spectators, who were informally sprawled along the sidelines on towels and in low-slung beach chairs watching the game in progress. As soon as it was over, Jason got Samantha and Andrea settled in, then strode on to the court.

Samantha knew little about volleyball. She had until now cultivated her ignorance. It was merely a game, she'd told herself. Child's play. She needed to know nothing more than that.

She was wrong.

It was demanding, gruelling, hot and exhausting. A child couldn't have done it. A moderately fit adult would have collapsed in no time. It required endurance, strength, incredibly quick reflexes, and teamwork. It reminded her of a ballet. Just as ballet taxed one's muscles, one's mind, one's stamina and often challenged one to create with a partner a harmonious whole, so, oddly enough, did playing volleyball.

It was a sobering thought. And, as Samantha watched Jason serve and spike and dig and set, as she watched him jump and plunge, as she watched him respond immediately, almost instinctively to whatever move Toby made, she couldn't help but acknowledge the beauty of the sport.

She couldn't help acknowledging the beauty of the man, either.

It was that as much as anything else which set her mind in a whirl. For, while she sat there, if her appreciation of Jason's sport grew, her appreciation of Jason, the man, grew even more.

Since she had arrived—no, since she had first met him in the parlour at the Rudley School—Samantha had been avoiding an examination of the physical Jason Cole. She had practically made a career out of pretending he wasn't there or, when forced to admit he was, of looking the other way—for all the good it had done her. But, short of closing her eyes for the whole afternoon, she could do that no longer.

So she watched and admired and hungered, her eyes following the curve of his spine as he leaped and spiked the ball, tracing the line of his arm as he flung himself head first to dig his opponent's spike out of the sand. She watched the way the sand clung to his damp back and hair-roughened legs and chest, she watched him wipe the sweat from his brow and shove his hair back off his forehead, she watched as beads of perspiration trickled down his chest and slid under the waistband of his shorts.

She swallowed, overheated herself, a steamy feeling that owed little to the Florida sun.

'Isn't Toby wonderful?' Andrea asked.

'Toby?' Samantha hadn't even noticed Toby was there. The physical Jason Cole had commanded every bit of her attention.

He spared her a bit, too. Though most of the time his mind was strictly on the game, every once in a while she caught him glancing her way, and during one time-out he gave her a heart-stopping grin. After a particularly hard-won point, after a mighty save, and finally, after the last bitterly fought victory of the afternoon was theirs, she found his eyes on hers. And she overheard one of the well-oiled 'volley dollies' say enviously to a friend, 'I wish he'd look at *me* like that.'

Moments later there was even more to envy, for Jason, gritty, sweaty and sandy, walked right past the water bottle and straight over to Samantha, hauled her to her feet, into his arms, and gave her a hungry kiss.

'So, what do you think?' he asked her, wiping his face with a towel, then slinging an arm over her shoulders and hauling her against him.

Samantha gulped. 'Uh—very nice.'

He cocked a sardonic brow. 'Nice?' His voice was dry, mocking her, making her blush. She could feel the great gulping breaths he took.

'Well, you know I don't know——'

He grinned and ruffled her hair. 'Yeah, I know.' He hugged her hard against his side, tipped his head back and drained the water bottle Toby handed him. Then, still hanging on to Samantha, he started walking towards the sea. 'But I'm glad you came.'

'Me, too.'

He grinned at her. 'Cripes, I'm beat. I'm filthy, too. Probably shouldn't be touching you. C'mon. We'll swim. That'll help.'

Samantha stopped. 'Not me. You go ahead.'

Jason gave her an odd look.

'I'm not hot,' Samantha lied, slipping out of his grasp. 'I'll wait here.'

'But——'

Toby and Andrea were coming at a run down the beach towards them. Samantha couldn't imagine where Toby found the energy to run after all those games. Youth, she thought, feeling every bit of her twenty-four years as they splashed past her and Jason and dived, whooping, under the incoming waves.

'Sam,' Jason implored her, as his fingers caught hers.

She hung back, steadfast. 'You go ahead.'

'Won't she swim with you, Cole?' The flop-haired blond who'd invited her to the party last night gave them a mocking grin. 'Must be slipping.'

'Stuff it, Calhoun,' Jason gritted, but even as he did so he dropped Samantha's hand. 'I'll be right back. Wait for me,' he instructed. And turning, he strode off into the surf.

'I'll take ya in, sweetheart.' Calhoun gave her a broad wink.

Samantha shook her head. 'No, thanks.' She turned on her heel and walked back up to the rise, where she turned and sat down. Calhoun hadn't moved. However, when she pointedly looked past him, at last he gave a negligent shrug.

'Suit yourself.' He turned his back and ambled into the water.

Jason didn't stay in long and, when he came out, he came straight to Samantha. Local fans were still waiting to clap him on the back and shake his hand, complimenting him on the game, remarking on his skill. Jason talked to them easily, but all the while he kept moving up the beach.

Girls followed him with their eyes and, in some cases, with their feet. Jason was polite if they spoke, signed autographs, chatted briefly, but his grip was firm on Samantha's, and the looks some of the girls gave her could have knocked her flat.

She didn't need the looks of the girls to accomplish that. She was, in her present frame of mind, capable of falling over simply from the circumstances. Whoever would have imagined she'd be walking hand in hand up the beach with a man like Jason Cole?

Certainly not Dena McGarvey. She'd left messages by the dozen at the hotel desk while Jason had been out.

'Oh, cripes,' Jason said, his face going pale while Samantha's heart plummeted right to the floor.

Why did he say Dena didn't matter, then turn white when he heard her name?

A pain began to grow right where Samantha's heart used to be. She drew her hand out of Jason's and said tonelessly, 'You'd better call her.'

'Yeah.' Jason was heading for the nearest pay phone even as he spoke. He was almost out the door when he turned back. 'Wait for me.'

But Samantha couldn't. For all that he insisted that there was nothing between Dena and himself, his actions proved otherwise. The second his back was turned, she fled.

When she got to the suite, she flung herself on to the bed and buried her head in the pillow.

You stupid, stupid girl, she told herself over and over. How could you let yourself in for this? You knew. You knew!

But knowledge alone, she realised as she lay in silence, had not been enough to save her.

There was a rattle, the sound of a key turning in the lock.

Jason appeared at her bedside. 'What's wrong?' He had been smiling, but his smile vanished when he met her gaze.

'N-nothing.' She took a swipe at her hair, trying to straighten it, grateful that at least she hadn't let herself deteriorate into tears.

But Jason clearly didn't believe her. He sat down on the bed. Instinctively Samantha moved away.

'Hey.' His voice was soft, questioning. 'What's up?'

'Did you talk to Dena?' Samantha asked, her voice toneless.

Jason's face cleared momentarily. He seemed almost to breathe a sigh of relief. 'Yeah, I did.' He grinned. 'She's fine. Just wanted to tell me how pleased the new client was with her. She had a couple of hours of shots yesterday afternoon and some more this morning.'

That was all, huh? Samantha didn't believe it for a minute. A famous, talented woman like Dena McGarvey didn't leave a dozen phone messages just to say the day had gone well. Days like that for her were like days with half a dozen cello students for Samantha—nothing to call home about, and certainly nothing to call Florida about.

'I see.' She turned and stared out the window towards the ocean. Why didn't he just stop the charade and go away?

Instead he reached for her hand. 'Where were we?' he asked. His voice was husky, his eyes slumbrous.

Samantha put one hand against his chest and shoved. 'You were just coming up to get cleaned up. And I was going to get a magazine and read.'

Jason looked at her, taken aback. 'But, Sam——'

'No. Please, Jason, don't!'

Just don't, she begged him silently. Even now, with Dena McGarvey in the forefront of her mind, it was still hard to resist him. No man should have so much power and so few scruples.

'Sam——'

'No!'

Whether he would have persisted further, Samantha was relieved not to have to find out. At that moment there was laughter and talking in the living-room, and seconds later, Andrea appeared in the doorway.

'Oh, sorry,' she said when she saw her brother and Samantha sitting on the bed. She began to back quickly out of the room.

'No, that's all right.' Samantha jumped to her feet. 'I'm sure you want to get cleaned up. I'm the only one who doesn't have to, since I'm the only one who didn't swim. I'll just take my magazine and go down by the pool. See you later.'

Before any of them could say a word, she fled.

There were only a few people in the pool when she sat down, but shortly they were joined by several of the players and an equal or even greater number of women, who hung on them and squealed or giggled.

One or two of the players hailed her, but, beyond a brief nod of acknowledgement, Samantha paid them no heed. She bent her head over the magazine and pretended a fascination with European autumn fashion that would have astounded anyone who knew her. It certainly would have amazed Jason, who still felt it necessary to comment every day that she wore one of his T-shirts instead of one of her original blouses with the billowing sleeves.

And there she was, thinking about Jason again. Drat!

All of a sudden there was a sharp tug on her braid and a body dropped on to the *chaise-longue* next to hers. 'Hi there.'

Startled, Samantha looked over to see the flop-haired blond. 'Oh—er—hello...Mr Calhoun, isn't it?'

'Just call me Bart, Sammie.'

'Samantha.' She started to say her name frostily, but just then Jason, Toby and Andrea came around the corner of the building. Her voice cracked and the word came out slightly husky. Still unable to face Jason with the sort of equilibrium she felt she needed, Samantha deliberately looked away from them and gave Bart Calhoun a wide smile.

He knew encouragement when he saw it. He winked and took her magazine from her hands, setting it on the flagstone patio. 'That's better. I wondered if you weren't playing hard to get. I think it's about time we got acquainted, don't you?'

'That...might be nice.' Samantha swallowed carefully. She had no desire to get acquainted with Bart Calhoun, but she had a tremendous desire to snub Jason Cole. The latter won out.

Jason stopped next to her *chaise-longue*. 'Let's go to dinner.'

'I'm not really hungry.'

Jason frowned. 'I made a reservation for four.'

Samantha shrugged. 'So change it.'

His frown deepened and he gave her an arch look, let his eyes drift to Andrea, then fastened his gaze back on her. The import of the message was clear: it's part of your job.

Samantha bristled. He had played that game once too often. 'I'm *not* hungry,' she said vehemently. 'I do not want to go and eat. You can "chaperon" for once. I think I'm allowed a few hours off once in a while.' This last was said through clenched teeth.

The moment she spoke, she regretted it, for Andrea looked positively stricken.

'I didn't mean——' she began, reaching out for Andrea's hand.

But Jason jerked his sister away. 'By all means, stay here, then, Ms Peabody,' he said, his tone scathing. 'We wouldn't want you to file charges for overwork.' He strode off, dragging Andrea after him and with Toby trailing at his heels.

Bart Calhoun let out a low whistle. Samantha squirmed uncomfortably and reached down to try to retrieve her magazine. But Bart was quicker and held it out of her reach.

'I thought we were getting acquainted.'

Sighing, Samantha folded her hands in her lap. She could hardly make a mad dash for the room the moment Jason left.

She found out more about Bart Calhoun over the next hour and a half than she ever wanted to know. He was glib, pushy and on the border of obnoxious, but Samantha bore up under it because she felt she deserved it. She had, in trying to get back at Jason, hurt Andrea's feelings a great deal. No matter how angry she was at

Andrea's brother, she never should have done that.
Andrea was young and sensitive. She counted Samantha
as a friend, and Samantha had been inexcusably rude.
Forcing herself to listen to Bart Calhoun detail his enormously successful skill on the volleyball court and to
have to watch him at least attempt to demonstrate his
incomparable skill with the 'dollies'—notably her—was
a small penance to pay for her sin.

He went on and on, punctuating his accounts with
swigs of beer. He offered Samantha one. She wanted to
refuse, but didn't. She got the feeling it would be safe
to say no to Bart Calhoun some of the time, but not all.

Since she wasn't going swimming with him if he asked,
and she certainly wasn't going to bed with him when he
asked—she had no doubt at all that he would—she decided the safest thing to acquiesce to was a beer.

She sipped hers while he gulped his, downing four to
her one, which was still half-full when he decided it was
time to take a dip.

'Come with me,' he commanded, holding out an imperious hand.

'No, thank you.'

He scowled. 'Don't be a stick-in-the-mud, Sammie.'

'I'm not. I just...don't want to swim.'

Bart sighed and looked as if he was going to do more
than argue when a soft voice stopped him.

'I'll swim with you, sweetie.' One of the dollies appeared at his side and ran her hand up his arm.

'You will, huh?' Bart's voice became instantly seductive. Samantha might as well have turned to stone
where she sat.

'Oh, yes,' the girl cooed. 'I'd looooove to.'

Samantha cheered silently. Go to it, sugar. And she
couldn't have been happier when the flaxen-haired girl
tugged Bart over to the pool's edge, then teetered help-
lessly and pulled him in with her.

The horseplay began then and, relieved, Samantha went back to her magazine. Things were working out all around. At least, she thought they were until Bart hoisted himself out of the water and came to stand over her.

'Your turn.'

Samantha looked up. 'No, thanks.'

'Got to,' Bart said. 'Can't come 'round here 'less you swim.' He slurred the words and Samantha began to think that exercise on top of all the beer he had drunk was having a distinct effect on his sobriety.

'Why don't you sit down again?' She nodded towards the *chaise-longue*.

'Whyn't you come to bed with me?' he countered, giving her a leer.

Samantha flushed and looked down. 'Quit that.'

A strong hand reached down and grasped her wrist. 'No way, sweetheart. You swim or you come to bed.'

Samantha struggled against him, casting a desperate glance around for the girl who had saved her last time. But whoever she was, she had apparently lost interest in Bart for she was nowhere to be seen. 'Let go!'

But Bart ignored her except to say, 'You wanna wrestle, we can do it better in my bed.'

'I don't want——' Samantha began, but then,

'Hey, Cole,' she heard him yell towards the man just coming in the gate. 'Watch this. Your girlie will swim with me!'

'No! Please, no!' Samantha screamed.

But words meant nothing, for the next moment Bart grabbed her around the waist, lifting her. Then she flew through the air, sensed the sudden cold, and—oh, no!—felt the water closing over her head.

CHAPTER EIGHT

'HELP!' Samantha floundered to the surface momentarily, only to submerge again. 'Hel——'

It was exactly the way she remembered it. Twenty years had passed, and nothing had changed. Not the sucking suffocation, the wavering blue world, the searing in her lungs, the press of panic on her brain.

And then strong arms were lifting her, holding her. 'It's all right.'

'No! I——' Instinctively she fought for breath.

'Sam! I said, it's all right.'

'J—Jason?' Still she scrabbled against him.

'Hold still!' He sounded furious. She felt his arms tighten around her, crushing her against him, and then he was dragging her to the side of the pool. She gripped him desperately, her nails digging into his shoulders, but for the first time since she'd hit the water the panic receded; she felt safe.

The feeling was premature. Jason boosted her up into Bart's waiting grasp, then hauled himself out after.

She was in Bart's arms for only a moment before Jason pulled her back and thrust her at Toby. 'Take care of her,' he barked, then whirled to confront Bart. 'What in hell did you think you were doing?'

'I didn't think——' Bart began backing away.

Jason lunged at him. 'You bloody well didn't! Lord almighty, man, you might have drowned her!' His fist drew back, but, before he could do a thing, Samantha wrested herself from Toby's grasp.

'No! Stop it!' She flew at Jason, clinging to his arm. 'Don't! Please don't! He didn't know! I should have said!'

Jason still looked murderous. 'Damn it, Samantha! How can you defend——?'

'Stop it!' she commanded, getting a grip on herself. 'Don't act like a Neanderthal! I'm all right. You saved me. I'm *all right*.' She glared at Jason, shaking.

He dropped his arm, with her still hanging on it like a dead weight. His eyes raked her. He was scowling, still angry. 'You're saying this is *your* fault?'

'Well, I——'

Jason's jaw set in a hard line. 'All right then, Ms Peabody. I guess we know how to fix things, don't we?'

Samantha blinked. 'What do you mean? It only happened because I didn't say I couldn't swim. If I'd said——'

'Or if you could swim.'

'Well, I can't, so——'

'Yet. Starting tomorrow we remedy that situation. You learn.'

Samantha felt the familiar panic welling. 'To swim? Me? Oh, no.' She started backing away. 'I can't. I——'

'You will. Employer's orders.' The hardness of his eyes and the stoniness of his face told her he meant exactly what he said.

'But you hired me to teach cello, to be Andrea's chaperon, not...'

'Being her chaperon means being with her,' Jason informed her smoothly. 'I let you sit on shore all the time because I figured you just didn't want to swim. I didn't know you couldn't.'

'And now that you know, of course, you have to make a big deal out of it?' Samantha said bitterly. She was shivering, less from cold than from panic. Her teeth began to chatter.

'Now that I know, I'm going to rectify the situation.'

'I don't *want* to swim!'

'Well, *I* want you to be able to protect yourself. In case anything like this——' he fixed Bart with a hard glare '—happens again. And in case Andrea gets in trouble, I'd like to know you can help her out.'

'But——'

'You're learning to swim, Sam,' he told her flatly. 'Starting in the morning.'

'You won't be able to find a teacher by morning.'

He gave her a tight smile and poked his chest. 'You want to see your teacher? You're lookin' at him.'

'Let's go.'

Samantha opened one eye and promptly shut it again.

A hand jiggled her shoulder lightly but firmly. 'Sam, I said, let's go.'

She tried to shrug the hand off, but it clung persistently. And, when she still didn't respond, seconds later the covers were ripped right off.

'Hey!' She sat bolt upright, clutching her flimsy nightgown to her breasts as she scrambled to cover herself again.

'It's time for your lesson,' Jason said mildly. He held the sheet in his fist, and he wasn't relinquishing it.

Samantha, who hadn't thought she could feel sicker at the prospect, immediately did. 'Jason,' she protested. 'Please.' He couldn't do this to her. He simply couldn't.

Jason waited, blue eyes glinting dangerously. Then he beckoned to her. Samantha shrank back against the pillows, glaring at him. He stared back, impervious to the negative set of her jaw. His eyes had other things to occupy themselves with. She shivered.

'Give me that,' she commanded, trying again to snatch the sheet from him, but Jason shook his head and dragged it off the bed entirely.

'Five minutes, Sam. Get your suit on or I'll take you like that.' Then, turning on his heel, he went out the door, sheet in hand.

Just like yesterday, she thought glumly. Only yesterday it had merely been a walk he'd requested.

She couldn't do it, just couldn't. Maybe if she explained. She had never explained to anyone before, but she'd never been pushed this hard either. And Jason wasn't unreasonable. Was he?

She got out of bed, stripped off the nightgown and pulled on a pair of shorts and a T-shirt.

Jason spun around with an approving look when the door opened. The approval turned to a frown when he saw what she was wearing.

'I can't do it, Jason,' she began quickly. 'You don't understand.'

For a moment he didn't reply. Then he said, 'So explain it to me.'

'I——'

'But put your suit on first.'

She sighed. 'Jason, please...'

'Look, I'll listen. I promise. But you have to promise me to put your suit on.'

Stalemate.

Toby gave a muffled snore and rolled over on the sofa bed. Outside the window an early riser started his car. Jason didn't budge.

Stymied, Samantha gave a tiny shrug. 'If you insist.'

He nodded.

Samantha went back in the bedroom and got into her suit. It was a modestly cut one-piece in bright blue. A NetWork suit. Flattering. Sexy, almost, she thought nervously as she stood in front of the floor-length mirror.

It delineated a lot more of Samantha Peabody than her shapeless skirts and roomy blouses ever had. Whether that was good or bad, she wasn't quite certain. Sighing, still nervous, she went back out to join Jason.

They walked to the pool in silence. It was scarcely six o'clock, but already the day was warm. It would be a scorcher on the beach, even with the breeze off the ocean. Samantha didn't envy Jason his day's work. It didn't seem so simple any more. If she were he, she would be getting as much sleep as she could.

She said as much, and Jason shook his head. 'I can sleep on the plane home.'

When they reached the side of the pool, he sat down on the edge, dangling his legs in the water. Samantha hung back.

He patted the concrete next to him. 'Sit down.'

Samantha looked suspiciously at the water, then let her gaze drift hopefully back to the *chaises-longues* which were all empty and looked far more comfortable. Jason ignored the hint and patted the concrete again. Reluctantly Samantha sat, keeping her feet tucked under her, staring down at her hands. Jason waited.

She swallowed. 'It's going to sound stupid.'

He didn't speak, but his eyes were gentle.

Samantha took a deep breath. 'I was barely four years old. We were in France, staying with friends of Daddy's. They had a château with a huge swimming-pool. They also had a little boy named Etienne who was somewhat of a roughneck.'

'A Neanderthal?' Jason's mouth quirked at one corner.

Samantha smiled. 'Yes, actually. He was older than I was. Maybe six. Etienne thought it was great fun to tease me, and——' she shrugged awkwardly '——I guess I reacted to being teased even then. He thought of horrible stories and told them to me because I believed them.

He chased me.' She shook her head at the memories. What a sissy she had been.

'One day he chased me and, when he caught me, he...threw me in the pool.' She shuddered even now as she remembered. 'I couldn't swim. He couldn't get me out. He tried.' She swallowed hard. Her fingers knotted. 'It was just luck one of the gardeners found us. We both nearly drowned.'

'Stupid kid,' Jason muttered. Then he scowled. 'But I guess it happens. Why didn't they teach you to swim after that, though?'

'They tried.' That memory made Samantha shudder, too. 'My father did, anyway, right then. He said anyone could swim. All I needed to do was practise.' She stared out across the still blue water, remembering. 'So he threw me in again.'

'What?'

Samantha nodded jerkily. 'It was supposed to be so simple. You just float, he said. I didn't. So he...tried it again.' Her voice became a bare whisper as she remembered first the fear and then the failure. 'And again.'

'Good lord.' Jason went totally silent then, staring not at Samantha but at the pool in which his legs were dangling. The expression of horror on his face told her exactly what his mind was seeing—the same thing hers had seen every time she let herself dwell on those memories at all: blue water sucking her down, closing over her head. Panic. Desperation. And failure. Always failure.

'I never did learn.' She looked off towards the palmettos just barely stirring in the morning breeze. 'I won't even go near the water now. I never have. At least, not until last night.'

'It's not your fault. I don't know how the hell anybody could learn, taught like that.' Jason's face was hard and angry, exactly the way her father's face had looked when

he'd had to fish her out. The instant their eyes met, he
seemed to realise what his expression must be saying to
her for it softened at once. 'He's an idiot, your old man.'

'He's a brilliant man, a fantastic violinist. One of the
best in the world,' Samantha said.

'Maybe.' Jason shrugged. 'Not much of a father,
though.'

Samantha lifted her chin. 'You don't know that. He
took care of me for years. My mother left, not him.'

'She probably left because of him!'

'Jason!' Samantha stared at him, shocked.

His gaze slid away. 'Sorry. I'm just reacting. I think
he sounds like a jerk.'

'He's not.'

Jason just looked at her, then slowly shook his head.
He sat very still for a long while, his expression unreadable. Then he seemed to make up his mind, and he
slipped off the side into the waist-high water and held
out his arms to her. 'Come here.'

She shook her head. 'No. I can't. I told you.'

'Sam, you can stand here. I'll hold you.'

'I don't want to.'

'Don't you?' His voice was soft, persuasive, his blue
eyes hypnotic. 'Don't you want to just dangle your feet?
The water's cool. Lots nicer than the air.'

'I don't——'

'Sam, trust me.'

The words were both command and plea. Jason's
hands were inches from hers. Strong, callused hands with
long, square-tipped fingers. Samantha had always loved
looking at Jason's hands, even when she'd first thought
they were a piano-player's hands. They seemed so
capable, whether they were stirring up scrambled eggs,
spiking a volleyball or picking out 'chopsticks'. She remembered the way just yesterday they had held her close;

then she tried to forget. She didn't want to think of Jason
that way.

But she couldn't put it out of her mind. She remembered, too, that last night in the pool they had promised
a security she had never known. In other areas she might
be a fool to trust him. But she also knew that she could
trust him about this.

She put her hands in his.

Slowly, gently, he drew her down into the pool. It was
more than cool. It was almost cold as she slipped shivering into the still water. She gasped slightly at the feel
of it lapping against her breasts. But, before she could
do more, Jason pulled her against him so that they stood
snugly together. Their bodies rocked slowly back and
forth.

His hold was meant to be comforting, reassuring. And
in a way, it was. But it was also undeniably erotic.

So little separated them. The thin fabric of her suit,
the soft cotton of Jason's trunks. All the rest was skin
against skin. Smooth and supple against firm and hair-
roughened. Soft against hard. Warm flesh in cool water.
Burning. Hotter than hot.

Samantha felt more than security. She felt desire—her
own desire curling out, unfolding inside her, blossom-
ing, opening, and Jason's, urgent, strong, very hard. So
much so that in another moment he stepped back slightly
and looked down at her, his expression sheepish.

'And I said, trust me?' One corner of his mouth lifted.

Samantha looked up at him shyly, her cheeks burning
in confusion.

Jason sucked a deep breath and his hands tightened
on hers. 'I meant it,' he said, meeting her gaze. 'You
can trust me.'

And right now—right here—she knew she did.

They moved slowly, simply walking around the pool
first, gliding like sleepwalkers through the shallow end,

barely stirring the water. Jason ducked down periodically, submerging to the eyeballs and then blowing out great quantities of bubbles while he smirked at her, a dark wet fringe of hair in his eyes.

Samantha laughed. 'You look like a demented, lecherous alligator.'

He popped up again and showed her two rows of even white teeth in a broad grin. 'Funny you should notice.'

Samantha expected that he would be insisting that she do that same thing, but he never mentioned it. He just walked with her, talking all the time, telling her stories about when his father taught him to swim.

It had been a vastly different experience from her own, that was clear from the outset. She had never known Jason's father, but she thought she would have liked him. He sounded, from everything she'd heard, as if he had been a hard driver, but a kind man. Like his son? she wondered. But Jason was such an enigma, she wasn't sure.

'Time to get out,' he said suddenly.

Samantha was startled. 'What?'

'It's after eight. I've got to be at the court for semi-finals by nine.'

'Oh, sorry.' How could she have forgotten? Did she think he had come clear to Florida to spend all day simply walking around the shallow end of a swimming-pool with her? She followed him, chagrined and dripping, out of the pool.

Jason dried off quickly, and slung the towel around his neck. Samantha dried off more slowly. It felt strange to be doing it outside, stranger still to be doing it in the company of a man. In the company of Jason.

She flicked a quick glance at him and found him watching her. Quickly she looked away, wrapping the towel around her like a sarong.

He grinned at her defensiveness. 'You can still trust me, Sam,' he said. 'I've got a long day ahead.' Then he looped his arm over her shoulder and walked her back to the room.

Jason and Toby won the double elimination tournament at five-fifteen p.m. They received their award money at five-thirty, got interviewed by a television sports commentator at six, cleared out of the hotel by six-thirty, and were winging their way westward by quarter past seven.

'Clockwork,' Toby breathed once the aeroplane left the ground. 'You don't know how rare that is,' he said with a grin to Andrea.

'I hope to find out,' Andrea said and gave him a hopeful smile.

Samantha turned her head towards Jason, who was sitting on her other side, curious about his reaction.

Jason smiled. She gave him a half-smile in return, still not quite sanguine about the relationship between Andrea and Toby, but even less sanguine about her own relationship with Andrea's brother, a fact borne in on her anew seconds later when his hand covered hers and she stiffened and started to pull away.

'Don't panic.' There was the sound of gentle teasing in his voice.

She shot him a wary glance, but he just grinned silently and made no further moves.

It was a four-and-a-half-hour flight. For most of that time, her hand was in his. Even during dinner, he didn't entirely let go of her. And when at last they landed, as they walked down the tunnel from the plane, Jason still held her fingers firmly.

Mine, he seemed to say. She's mine.

But Dena was his, too, for when they landed, there she was.

'Jase!' She launched herself at him, giving him a bone-crushing hug and a smacking kiss. 'I'm so glad to see you.'

Samantha wrenched her hand away. But if Jason noticed, he didn't fuss. Dena snuggled against him and his arm looped over her shoulder, just as it had over Samantha's on the way to the plane in Florida. His attention was all on Dena.

Samantha, standing alone in the corridor, stared after them and asked herself, Well, what did you expect? Nothing really had changed.

'Hey, Sam.'

She blinked. Andrea and Toby had gone on ahead, but Jason had stopped and was looking back over his shoulder, his other arm still over Dena's. 'What're you waiting for? Come on!'

'I——'

He held out his free hand as if it would be the most natural thing in the world for her to take it. Samantha just looked at it, baffled, hurt. She looked at him with Dena on his other arm and wondered if the man had any notion of the chaos he created in her mind. Was it perfectly all right, in his lifestyle, to have two women at once? Did she even have to ask?

She sighed. 'Coming.'

Dena had brought Jason's Jeep to the airport. 'I thought you'd rather have a reception committee than take a taxi.'

'Sure.' He grinned, ruffling her hair.

Samantha, despite telling herself she shouldn't, felt a stab of jealousy so strong she felt like screaming out loud. Instead she bit her lip and shoved into the back with Toby and Andrea, while Jason drove and Dena climbed in beside him.

She wouldn't let her guard down again. Couldn't. No matter what. The moment Jason pulled up to the house, she was jumping out and heading for the door.

'Hey, Sam, what's the matter?' he called.

But Samantha shook her head, not turning. 'Nothing. Just tired, that's all.'

At one in the morning she could lie there no longer. She had tossed and turned, counted everything from sheep to violins to volleyballs, all to no avail.

Finally, despairing, she swung her legs out of the bed on to the floor, slipped her nightgown over her head and reached for a clean pair of shorts and a shirt. The night breeze that blew in through the window was cool and beckoning. She padded across the room and softly opened the door.

The house was dark and silent. She stood for a moment and stared out of the living-room window at the sand and the sea beyond. Then she reached for the doorknob. She didn't know where she was going, only knew that she had to gain a bit of perspective, to make some sense out of the mess that had become her life.

The moment she'd first seen Jason Cole, she'd recognised him as trouble. But had she turned and run? Not she! And now look at you, she berated herself. At least in May you knew what you wanted out of life and stood a chance of getting it. Now you know nothing and stand a chance of less.

She let herself out the front door, but had barely taken two steps when a voice spoke up from the shadows. 'Can't sleep?'

She whirled to see Jason in a director's chair at the far end of the porch, his feet up on the railing. He lifted his feet down and got up, giving her a rueful look. 'Neither could I.'

The mere sight of him, tired and slightly rumpled, set her heart to hammering, her immunity to crumbling. She raked a hand through her own dishevelled hair and began edging towards the steps. 'I—I just thought I might go for a walk.'

She expected he'd object. They both knew that lone women wandering about in the dead of night were possible prey to all sorts of unpleasantness. But he didn't. Before she knew it, he had taken her elbow and was leading her down the steps and across the Strand to the beach.

'You don't have to——'

'I do.' His voice brooked no argument. Nor did the firm grasp he had on her elbow as he towed her along. The night was cool, the breeze light. A three-quarter moon hung suspended over the ocean, throwing a streak of silver across the water and making ghostly shadows on the sand. Less than twenty-four hours ago they had done the same thing on a different ocean. Samantha was more confused than ever.

Jason led her straight down to the water. The tide was coming up, and before long cold water was rushing over Samantha's toes. She jerked back then, starting to pull away. But Jason hung on to her and just kept walking.

'Relax,' he said. His hand was firm on her arm, steady, reliable. Comforting, almost. Deceiving, Samantha thought.

'Where's Dena?' she asked deliberately.

Jason shrugged. 'Home, I should think.'

'You didn't go out with her?' She didn't know why she had to persist in this line of questioning. Some masochistic tendency, perhaps?

'No.'

'Is that why you couldn't sleep?'

His steps slowed slightly. 'No, Samantha,' he said after a moment, and his voice sounded almost mocking. 'That's not why I couldn't sleep.'

Samantha gritted her teeth at his patronising tone. Well, if that was the way he wanted it . . . 'Why couldn't you, then?'

'Guess,' he muttered.

Samantha looked at him more carefully. The moonlight etched the angles of his face in silver, making it seem harsh and uncompromising. Was he angry? If so, why? More to the point, at whom? Himself? Dena? Samantha?

The man was an enigma. Arrogant and teasing. Tender and gentle. Strong and vulnerable. If she had a million years, Samantha didn't think she would ever figure him out.

'Why couldn't you sleep?' he countered.

She shrugged indifferently, unable to confess the jealousy that Dena always seemed to spark in her.

'Ibañez?'

Samantha blinked. 'What?'

'I wondered if you couldn't sleep because you were worrying about Ibañez?'

She shook her head, relieved almost that he was so far off base. It made her glad that he didn't have an inkling of the myriad confused feelings she had about him. 'Not really. It's a great opportunity. She deserves it.'

'You deserve it,' Jason told her.

Samantha looked at him to see if he was teasing. He wasn't. She smiled, pleased that someone understood at least. 'Thank you.'

'You're welcome. Thank *you*.'

'For what?'

'For taking Andrea on. For teaching her. You've been everything she promised. And more.' He smiled at her

again, but in the moonlight his expression was serious.
'You're a wonderful teacher.'

'I love it,' she admitted.

'You're not really going to give it up, are you?'

'Well, Oliver and I...' The words sounded almost
strange on her lips. It seemed years since she had even
thought about Oliver.

Jason said a rude word. At least Samantha thought
he did, but it was muffled by the noise of the waves. He
started walking again, briskly now. She almost had to
run to keep up with him. 'You still don't have to stop
teaching,' he grated after a minute or two.

'Yes, I do.'

'Why?'

'I won't have time. I'll be busy.'

'Doing what?' he growled.

'Everything. Scheduling. Making reservations.
Keeping his wardrobe together. Smoothing the way.' She
gave a vague wave of her hand. 'There are always a
million things to do. Important things.'

'More important than teaching?' Jason persisted.

'I—well, yes.' But her voice didn't carry the zeal it
used to.

'You've developed a student to the extent that a man
like Raul Ibañez is willing to hear her, and you don't
want to keep teaching?'

'I didn't say I didn't want to——'

'Ah-ha!' He sounded as if he'd struck gold. 'You do
want to! So why don't you?'

'I told you!' Samantha cried.

'Oliver won't let you.' His voice was flat, almost
scornful.

'Oliver——!' she spluttered. 'It isn't a matter of what
he will and won't let me do! It isn't fair to him!'

'It sounds to me as if it isn't fair to you!'

Samantha shook her head fervently, angry now. 'You don't know anything about it! You don't know anything at all, Jason Cole. You don't understand music. You don't understand musicians. You don't understand me!'

She pulled away from him then and began to run back up the beach, stumbling, regaining her footing, hating herself for her outburst, hating him for getting to her and undermining her.

He caught her before she'd gone fifty yards. 'Sam! Stop, Sam!'

'Let me go!'

'No! Damn it, no! You've done nothing but run from me ever since the day we met! It's time to stop running.'

'Jason, no!'

'Samantha, yes.' There was a pause, a heartbeat. Then, 'It's time to face the music.'

Then he turned her in his arms and wrapped them around her, pressing her against him, letting her feel the hunger in him, the need. And then he was kissing her desperately.

This was the kiss that all his other kisses had been leading up to. It was the kiss that all her life Samantha knew she had been waiting for. The one that lifted her out of herself and fused her to a great reality—a reality in which Oliver faded, her father faded, all the cellos and flutes and violins in the world faded. A reality in which there was only need and time—and Jason.

They tumbled down on to the sand, their arms around each other. Jason's hands slid under her T-shirt, skimming up her ribs, easing inside her bra, stroking the soft flesh of her breasts, moulding them, massaging them. And Samantha moved against him, hesitation lost, fears obscured.

Her hands sought him, her lips tasted him, her body wanted him. It writhed under the subtle search of his fingers. She ran her own fingers up underneath his shirt, caressing his chest. His skin was hot to her touch, and she felt him tremble as her hands slid downwards again and brushed below the waistband of his shorts. He groaned, arching his hips against her.

The need in him should have frightened her. But if anything was frightening, it was that her own need was just as strong. She didn't think, just moved to accommodate him, settling back in the sand. And, when his fingers loosed the clasp of her bra, she felt only relief from its confinement. But then he touched her, his fingers sliding around and across her ribs, then stroking insistently, tantalisingly, across her breasts. The relief she'd felt gave way to stronger, more pleasurable sensations. Samantha moaned softly.

'I know what you mean,' Jason rasped. He tugged her T-shirt over her head and buried his face in the valley between her breasts. His soft hair brushed against her hot skin, and Samantha's hands came up to hold him close, her fingers tangling in his thick, tousled hair. She could have lain like this forever, sinking in sensations she'd never known existed, but Jason wouldn't let her. He took her further, working an unbelievable magic on her, making her his in every sense of the word.

She never thought to protest when he eased her shorts down her legs. She gasped, but in wonder, not in fear, when he shed his own clothes impatiently and came to kneel above her in the sand.

'Are you afraid, Sam?' he whispered at the sound of her whimper.

Samantha swallowed, then met his eyes and shook her head. How could you fear something so right, so beautiful? She could no more have turned away from Jason now than she could stop playing Bach in the middle of a piece. Like music that grew and wrapped itself around you until it became a part of you, this feeling, too, demanded a response for its completion.

Samantha held out her arms, and with a smile Jason came to her. The pain was sharp and swift, despite his attempt at gentleness, but Samantha didn't care.

She welcomed it, welcomed him. He had marked her, made her his, and in his loving she felt herself become a new creation.

Jason collapsed against her, his heart slamming, his face pressed into her neck as she felt him shudder and shiver and, finally, still.

And then she was Samantha Peabody again—daughter, teacher, striver, failure. But never again the same Samantha Peabody.

She was, lord help her, in love with Jason Cole.

CHAPTER NINE

'HAVE a focus, a purpose, a sense of direction,' Ambrose Peabody always told his daughter. And, for twenty-four years, Samantha had.

Now she felt as if she were in the centre of a whirling vortex, claimed by forces beyond her control, even beyond her reckoning. She knew she loved Jason Cole in spite of all her efforts not to. But knowing didn't help. She didn't have the faintest idea what to do now.

Love like this wasn't something she had even considered.

Whenever she had thought of love, she'd expected some gentle companionship, a bit of hearthside nurturing, a gentle glow—the sort of thing her father had always held up as the ideal, the sort she had anticipated with Oliver.

What she'd got was a forest fire, uncontrollable and unpredictable. It left her completely at a loss.

Worst of all was knowing that, regardless of how she felt, Jason was still wholly unsuitable, only interested in her as a momentary fling—another Fritz, but this time one she'd had the terrible judgement to fall in love with. For if one night Jason was loving her passionately, the next morning, when she got up, he was on the phone to Dena again, listening intently as if the fate of the world hung on her every word.

Samantha stood in the doorway watching him, watching the play of tenderness, sympathy, and love across his features, and she felt the pain of despair steal into her heart.

Jason didn't seem to see anything wrong with it. He sought her out the moment he got off the phone, coming up behind her, putting his arms around her and giving her a kiss.

Samantha jerked away. 'Stop it!' She wrapped her arms around herself.

He stepped back, his expression carefully blank. 'Sam?' His voice was soft, questioning.

'My name's not Sam,' she bit out. But her ears rang with the softly whispered 'Sam's, the gruff, aching 'Sam's that he had murmured last night. She wanted to cover her ears, to purge her mind, certain that in other circumstances he'd say 'Dena' the same way.

Jason just looked at her, his blue eyes flat and unreadable, his hands at his sides. 'Like that, is it?'

She faced him squarely and lied, 'Like that.'

Something flickered in his eyes. A muscle ticked in his jaw.

'Just like that,' Samantha repeated woodenly, and fled.

Jason worked out, played volleyball, lifted weights, went to meetings, talked on the phone, made momentous decisions and spent time with Dena. As the days and weeks passed, nothing seemed to change for him at all. Except that now he treated Samantha with kid gloves.

Several times he did try to approach her, to talk, to touch. But Samantha spurned every attempt. However much she had failed her father in all other respects, at least she knew now that she wasn't cut out for affairs.

Clearly Jason wasn't happy about that. If he had any frustration at all, it seemed to her to come from the fact that she wouldn't go to bed with him again. But no matter how much she might want to, Samantha couldn't bring herself to do that.

She had succumbed once. She had given in, had given him herself. He already had her heart, for what it was worth. But if she gave him her body night after night, she would end by giving him her soul.

And so she held him off. She made deliberate references to his 'Neanderthal' tendencies. She took to avoiding him whenever possible. She made the occasional disparaging remark. But even as she did so, she felt as if she were reliving Custer's last stand.

But, to her mind, he was luckier than she was. He could take out his frustration on the volleyball, whereas she could only take cold showers and play long, angst-filled sonatas on the cello.

And take it out he did. In Massachusetts, in Ohio, in Colorado, California, Illinois, and Wisconsin—wherever the tournament went through all of July and the first week in August—Jason played as if he was inspired.

Toby was as lithe and quick as ever, jumping and blocking, digging and spiking. But no one was a match for Jason. He slaughtered them all.

'At thirty-one, the old man of professional volleyball,' the *Los Angeles Times* called him. But he played with the skill of the best and the enthusiasm of the youngest week after week. Tirelessly and efficiently, all throughout the heat and humidity of the summer, he and Toby ploughed through opponent after opponent, while all Samantha and Andrea could do was watch.

It didn't matter to Andrea. She was as enthralled with the physical Toby Henning as she had ever been. She could sit enraptured for hours. But Samantha felt as if she were going to explode. She had no round white ball to bash, no sand to dive into head first, no exercise to take the edge off her desire.

The one thing that threw them together continually, however, was Samantha's swimming lessons. She would happily have stopped. They weren't in the least necessary, she argued. In fact—though she didn't say it—they were decidedly detrimental to her emotional health. But Jason insisted.

'Employer's orders,' he decreed once more. And he took her swimming every evening, no matter where they were.

It was a refined sort of torture for Samantha. She imagined—but didn't know if she hoped or not—that it was equally hard on him.

In any case, by the time they arrived in East Hampton the second weekend in August, she was an emotional wreck. They were, by invitation of one of her Rudley student's parents, making use of a house right on the beach at East Hampton. It was a blessing, Samantha thought, because another weekend with Jason in a cramped hotel suite was more than she could handle.

But even when Germaine's parents' house turned out to be big enough to house a political convention, Samantha wondered if it would be big enough for herself and Jason and all the feelings that were brewing between them. Especially when they arrived and, the moment they walked in the door, the phone rang and it was Dena.

Samantha slapped it into his hand and stalked off to find the bedrooms on her own. It was just as well, she thought. Lord knew she shouldn't be looking for bedrooms with Jason Cole!

Determinedly she picked the one furthest from the one that Toby put Jason's suitcase in. Then she lingered about upstairs until she had exhausted all possible avenues of interest before she at last went back down.

Jason was still on the phone. He gave her a vague smile and a slightly worried look as he held out his hand to her. But Samantha gave him a vague smile right back and walked on past.

'Sam,' he hissed at her, covering the receiver. But she kept right on walking out the french windows.

And when she came back an hour later, having walked into town, she knew what she had to do. She walked right in the door and rang up Oliver.

'Where were you?' Jason demanded. He loomed in the doorway, bare-chested, wearing only a pair of low-slung jeans. He was scowling at her.

Samantha looked away. 'Out.'

'You could have waited. We could have had your lesson.'

She shrugged. 'I can swim now, Jason. Anyway, I didn't know how long you'd be.'

'Not long,' Jason said tersely. 'We could still go.'

'No.' She turned away. The phone was beginning to ring.

'Calling Ibañez?' he persisted.

'No.'

He glowered at her. 'Who, then?'

'What business is it of yours?'

'You work for me.'

Samantha gave him a baleful stare. 'Do I?' Not for long. If she was lucky maybe she could even leave with Oliver this weekend. She turned away again.

'Damn it, Samantha!'

There was no answer in Oliver's room. 'Could you leave a message for him to call me, please,' Samantha said to the receptionist. She gave her name and number, then hung up.

'Archer.' Jason's voice was flat.

Samantha nodded. 'That's right.'

'Why?' He sounded belligerent.

'So I can arrange a time to see him,' Samantha said calmly.

'What for?'

'Because I want to.' She *needed* to. She could hardly remember what he looked like.

'What about Ibañez?'

'What about him?'

'When are you seeing him with Andrea?'

'I've arranged that already. I'm meeting him tomorrow at noon with Andrea.'

'Noon? I'm playing then.'

'So?' She had avoided watching him play as much as possible. But sometimes he insisted, dragging out his 'employer's rights' clause. At least with Ibañez he couldn't do that.

The scowl turned to a glare. 'I suppose you'll see what's-his-name after?'

'Oliver,' Samantha said sweetly. Jason snarled. 'It depends,' she went on. 'His first concert is tomorrow night. He'll be very wrapped up in getting ready for that in the afternoon. But later——' she nodded '—yes, I expect so.'

Jason grunted, scowling out the window towards the beach beyond.

'What's the matter?'

He stuffed his hands into the pockets of his jeans. 'Nothing.' And he turned on his heel and stalked out.

Samantha expected he would be around at supper, but he and Toby had gone out.

'Toby said they didn't want to bother us while we were practising,' Andrea told her as she rummaged through the refrigerator and put Germaine's parents' leftovers out for supper.

Good, Samantha thought. She couldn't think about him now. She needed to concentrate on getting Andrea primed for the next day's audition. She was as nervous about it as Andrea was. A successful audition would justify her summer as nothing else would. It would prove that in one way, at least, she could be a success.

They were halfway through the piece Andrea was going to play for Ibañez when the phone rang. Samantha left Andrea playing and went to answer it.

'Sammie, love, is that you? I just got your message.'

'Oliver!' Samantha wanted to throw her arms around him. He sounded so familiar. 'When can I see you?'

'Well...' he considered. 'Not tomorrow, certainly. I'm in rehearsal all day. And I'm dining with Wysocki. You know, the conductor. But in the evening, after the concert...?'

'Wonderful,' Samantha said, jumping on it. 'I'm looking forward to it.'

'Of course. Isn't it stupendous how all this has worked out? You, me, your father... I've got tons to tell you,' Oliver went on. 'The reviews have been magnificent. I know you'll want to see them.'

'Of course.'

'We can go over them together. You should have heard what Kilburne said in the *Post*.'

'Yes. I want to.' Samantha debated a moment, then added, 'I missed you.'

There was a second's startled silence. 'What? Oh, yes. I've missed you, too. No one has done right by my tux since I left New York, believe me. Ah, I see Nell waiting. See you tomorrow, love.' And he rang off, leaving Samantha staring at the receiver in her hand.

'Oliver?' a gruff male voice guessed.

She looked up to see Jason standing there, frowning at her. She didn't know when he'd come in. Stiffening, Samantha nodded.

'You're seeing him?'

'Yes.' She lifted her chin. 'Tomorrow night. After the concert.'

Jason's jaw tightened. He nodded curtly, his blue gaze arresting her as she turned to go back to Andrea.

'Samantha?' His voice halted her when she was almost out of the room.

'What?'

'Can you get an extra ticket?'

Samantha stared. 'Why?'

'I'd like to come.'

The audition with Raul Ibañez was supposed to be the Mount Everest of the weekend. But it became the mole-hill of Samantha's day.

Expecting little, merely doing a favour for his wife's old friend, Raul Ibañez was tremendously impressed by the talent of Andrea Cole.

'She plays well. The mechanics are good, yes? But more, she has soul.' He gave Andrea a slight smile, but directed his remarks to Samantha. *'Verdad?'*

Samantha nodded. It was true. She had mechanics herself, but she'd never had the depth of interpretation that to Andrea seemed to come naturally.

Ibañez blessed her with a smile. *'Ha tenido una profesora buena.* A very good teacher indeed.'

Samantha felt as if she could walk on air.

There was a long silence; then almost diffidently Ibañez went on. *'Me permite enseñarle?'*

Samantha looked startled. 'You want to teach her?'

'Con su permiso.' He nodded.

With her permission? Samantha almost fainted. 'I would b-be honoured,' she stammered.

Ibañez smiled and rubbed his hands together. *'Bueno.* You will come to me in the autumn?' he said to Andrea. 'I will be living in Los Angeles then. It will suit, no?'

Andrea nodded jerkily. 'Oh, yes.'

'You will have much work. *Mucho trabajo. Le gusta trabajar?'*

'Er—yes.'

He nodded again, pleased. *'Bueno.* We start now.' Another glance at Samantha. 'You listen.'

It wasn't a question. Samantha who, in the back of her mind, had known that, despite what she'd told Jason, she intended to go to the volleyball tournament to at least feast her eyes on him one last time, had the choice taken out of her hands.

If she felt a faint disappointment, she told herself she needed to get used to it. There was no future in it. No hope. And the sooner she got accustomed to life without Jason, the better off she would be.

They found Jason pacing the floor when they got back. 'It's past five. Where the hell have you been?' he snarled.

Startled, Samantha stared at him. 'I—with Andrea at Raul Ibañez's, of course.'

'The whole afternoon?'

'Yes.'

'He wants me as a student.' Andrea flung herself into his arms. 'Isn't that wonderful?'

Jason looked at Samantha over his sister's head. For a moment he didn't speak. Then, seeing Samantha's almost tremulous smile, he began to smile himself.

'Yeah. Yeah, it is. It's wonderful.' He gave Andrea a warm hug. Then his eyes went to Samantha again. 'Starting when?'

'Autumn.'

'Not right away?'

'No.' She wished it were. It would give her an excuse to leave that much sooner.

But Jason clearly didn't agree. He nodded, smiling. 'That's all right, then.'

Samantha looked at him, confused, but he didn't elaborate. He just got to his feet. 'Well, go get dressed up. We'll have dinner out before the concert.'

Samantha, thinking he meant to celebrate Andrea's triumph, agreed at once and vanished up the steps.

When she came back down, freshly showered and shampooed and wearing a mango-coloured gypsy dress that made her look tanned and glowing, she found only Jason waiting for her. He was wearing a dark suit, a pristine white shirt and a muted striped tie. He looked stern and elegant and powerful—the man that Samantha had feared way back in May. She didn't know who she feared more now—him or herself.

'Where are Andrea and Toby?' she demanded.

'Oh, you know kids. They'd rather have a Burger King.'

'I doubt they'll find one in East Hampton,' Samantha said tartly.

But Jason only grinned. 'I'm sure they'll manage. We'll meet them at the concert.'

He offered her his arm and she hesitated. But when he didn't move, reluctantly she took it. It was the first time she had touched him outside her swimming lessons since the night they had made love. And the tender warmth with which he touched her, the solicitousness with which he treated her, the gentle smiles that he gave her as they got in the car and drove to the restaurant made her want to cry.

Jason seemed quieter, too. More subdued. He made a valiant effort to ask questions about the afternoon—about Andrea, about the audition with Ibañez, about what would happen from here. But there was a strain between them, a tension that seemed to grow as the meal went on.

'Did you play all right today?' Samantha asked him finally, trying to guess the reason for his seriousness.

Jason paused, cutting his steak. 'We're still in winners' bracket. Why?'

'I just . . . wondered.'

'Do you care?' He was buttering a roll and he didn't look at her as he spoke.

'Of course I care.' Do you? she wanted to ask him.

But Jason just took a bite of the roll, looking less than convinced.

Samantha put it down to exhaustion. She knew enough about his weekends of 'play' now to know they were anything but. 'Are you sure you want to go to this concert tonight?' she ventured finally when they were almost done with eating.

'Why? Do you think I'm too much of a Neanderthal to appreciate it?' Jason's voice was hard.

'Of course not, I——'

He shoved back his chair. 'Are you done? Then let's go.'

The tickets Oliver had provided were halfway back and far to the left. She remembered he had promised her 'front and centre' seats, and wondered if the location was an indication of Oliver's relative worth. Or perhaps her worth to him.

Jason didn't seem to care. Samantha expected that he might sleep through the entire programme. But, in fact, he was singularly attentive, especially when her father and Oliver played.

He leaned forward in his chair, scowling intently as her father was introduced. He clapped politely, but his gaze narrowed and, to Samantha at least, his disapproval was evident. But it was nothing compared to the way he looked at Oliver. He looked at Oliver the way a rabid dog eyes the postman.

Samantha was looking at Oliver with new eyes, too. It was the first time she'd seen him since May, and she found herself trying to find in him the man she had wanted to marry scant months ago.

He played as well as he ever did, his virtuosity evident, his tones as pure as crystal as they rippled into the silent auditorium. He was still beautiful, too—his blond hair gleaming almost silver in the spotlights, his tuxedo immaculate, his bright red cummerbund providing just the right impression of dash and impetuosity to contrast with the stark black of his coat and the glacial white of his pleated shirtfront.

He didn't look as if he ever worried, was ever messed up, had ever sweated a drop. He looked, as always, like an angel, not a man.

And he didn't stir her senses in the least.

Samantha ventured a quick glance at the man beside her and found it hard to believe that he and Oliver were even of the same species. There was a hard, rough, masculine vitality about Jason, even sitting still as stone, that Oliver had never even dreamed of.

For most of her twenty-four years, Samantha hadn't dreamed of it either. Now she couldn't help but make the comparison. And, when she made it, Oliver seemed sadly lacking. A tame house-cat alongside a panther, a girl scout campfire compared to an all-out conflagration.

She wouldn't get burned with Oliver, though, Samantha reminded herself.

It was not the consolation she'd hoped for.

Jason sat rigidly for the whole time Oliver was playing. His eyes moved restlessly back and forth from Samantha to Oliver. And when at last Oliver's piece was over and the applause came in thunderous waves, he managed half a dozen claps before dropping his palms into his lap.

'Not your sort of music?' Samantha guessed.

Jason shrugged.

'He's very good,' she said, feeling somehow that Oliver needed defending.

Another shrug. Muscular shoulders moved easily within the confines of a superbly tailored coat. Samantha looked away.

'I must go. I'm meeting him backstage,' she said quickly.

'I'll come.'

'You needn't bother.'

'I want to.' And he shadowed her like a sheepdog with a stray.

Despairing of being able to shake him, Samantha plunged ahead. Music and musicians weren't his thing. He would get bored soon enough. Then maybe he would go and call Dena.

She found her father first. He stood just inside the reception-room as she and Jason were borne in with a crowd of enthusiastic concert-goers. When Samantha approached, Ambrose gave her a slightly distracted look, as if he thought he recognised her, but wasn't sure from where.

'Daddy,' she said and put her arms around him.

'Oh.' He smiled then, obviously relieved. 'Yes. Samantha, it's you.' He patted her awkwardly, then stepped back and surveyed her from top to toe, taking in her gypsy dress, her glowing tan, her bright smile. 'Nice to see you.' Then he turned his gaze on the man at her side.

The vague expression of approval faded like disappearing ink. Ambrose Peabody's eyes narrowed as he took in Jason's broad shoulders, his strong jaw, his torso, which looked muscular even within the confines of his suit coat. 'Who's this?'

'My name is Jason Cole,' Jason said before Samantha could reply.

'The brother of my student,' she supplied quickly, wanting to make the connection quite clear. She knew exactly what her father would think the moment he laid eyes on Jason.

'The brother of...ah, yes.' Ambrose looked faintly relieved. He gave Samantha a searching look, as if trying to discern signs of her mother in her. Samantha squirmed under his gaze, and felt her own relief when at last, satisfied, he turned away to accept more congratulations.

'Glad to see you, isn't he?' Jason said under his breath.

'Of course he is. He's just basking in his moment of glory,' Samantha said sharply.

'Oh, of course.'

She shot him a steely glance which he met with an equally steely smile. 'You don't have to stay, you know,' she said pointedly.

'I'm staying.' And that was that.

Then, all at once, arms came around her from behind and a wet mouth delivered a smacking kiss on her ear. 'Sammie, love!' And she turned to see Oliver's beautiful, mobile mouth beaming at her. He leaned in and nibbled at her ear again.

'Ah, Oliver!' She turned in his arms and gave him a hug, which he returned.

'Oliver!' Ambrose brightened perceptibly. 'How was your summer? China was marvellous, simply marvellous. We must have a chat.'

'Tonight?' Oliver suggested.

Ambrose frowned. 'I expected you'd want to spend tonight with Samantha.'

'Oh—er—yes. Absolutely.' Another peck and nibble, this time accompanied by a squeeze.

'She's spending it with me,' Jason said, his tone hard.

Oliver straightened, his eyes narrowing as he assessed for the first time the man on Samantha's left. His lower lip went out petulantly. He looked amazed, but no more so than Samantha at the proprietorial tone they'd just heard.

'Who are you?' Oliver demanded.

'This is—uh—Jason Cole, Andrea's brother,' Samantha told him quickly.

'Oh, right. The volleyball player.' Oliver dismissed him at once. 'Well, Sammie love, I'm sure he'll excuse you for one evening. We have a lot to catch up on,' Oliver said.

Jason turned to Samantha. 'Bring him along if you have to, but we're leaving.'

Samantha opened her mouth to protest. One look at Jason's face and she shut it again. Why he was behaving this way, she didn't know. What she did know was that she'd go along with it unless she wanted a scene.

She shrugged awkwardly. 'Are you sure you won't come, too, Daddy?'

Ambrose looked startled. 'No, of course not. You know I need my sleep.' He started to move away, then tapped Oliver's arm. 'First thing in the morning, my boy. We'll meet for breakfast. See you before I leave, my dear?' This last was directed to Samantha.

'Yes, of course. I want to tell you about my teaching. Raul Ibañez heard Andrea and——'

'Yes, of course,' Ambrose said, and before she could say any more he'd turned and got into a conversation with the concert-master.

'Well, if you're sure you won't come out just with me...' Oliver said to Samantha.

Jason stepped between them. 'She's working tonight.'

'Working?' Oliver almost yelped.

'Her time is mine.' Jason's eyes flashed fire.

Samantha looked at him warily. It was a side of him she hadn't seen but had predicted. The corporate takeover side. She swallowed hard.

He and Oliver stared at each other, neither moving as the crowds swirled and eddied around them. At last, 'I'll fetch my jacket and join you, then,' Oliver said.

Jason grunted, already moving towards the door, hauling Samantha along in his wake.

'You're very...' she began, then faltered, not knowing what to say.

'Yes,' Jason retorted tersely. 'I am.'

Samantha swallowed. 'I'm sorry my father was rather—er—preoccupied,' she ventured, wondering if that had contributed to his foul mood. 'He gets that way sometimes.'

Jason snorted. 'Sometimes?'

'Well, when he's extremely busy, he hates distractions.'

Jason nailed her with a stare. 'Like his daughter?'

Samantha felt her face flame. 'It—it's just the way he is.'

'Now that I believe,' Jason said harshly. 'What I don't believe is that you stand for it!'

'He's my father. He raised me. He loves me.'

'Does he? He has a funny way of showing it.'

Samantha would have argued with him, but she didn't have a chance to say anything else before Oliver joined them. 'What about Toby and Andrea?' she asked once they reached the car.

'Andrea said Ibañez wanted her to meet his wife. He'll bring them home.'

'Toby, too?' Samantha debated getting in the back and letting Oliver sit up front with Jason, then decided it was a poor idea. The more distance she got between the two of them, the better.

'Toby, too.' Jason started the car.

'It's a bit crowded on the knees back here,' Oliver complained.

'You'll live,' Jason said and shot out of the car park.

The distance wasn't long, but it seemed a million miles to Samantha. Jason might as well have been the Sphinx for all he contributed to the conversation, while Oliver chuntered on about the standing ovation he'd received in Asheville, the fantastic reception he'd got in Williamsburg, and the encores he'd done at Hilton Head.

'You should have been there,' he told Samantha while they idled at a traffic light.

'Yes.' She wondered if he even remembered that she might have been if he hadn't decided she 'distracted' him.

'Well, at least you heard me tonight.' He leaned forward and gave her shoulder a conciliatory pat.

Jason shot away from the light with unnecessary enthusiasm, jerking Oliver backwards in his seat.

It didn't stop him, however. Nothing stopped him. He continued his monologue all the way back to the house. Once there, he paused long enough to agree to a glass of wine when Samantha suggested it upon their arrival, then he sank into a *chaise-longue* on the deck overlooking the beach, and kept talking in a loud voice while she fetched the wine.

Jason stood glowering at him from the railing.

'Do you want a glass, too?' Samantha asked him, more as a matter of politeness than because she thought he'd take it. He never drank on tournament weekends. So she was not surprised by his curt, 'No.'

But she was astonished when he brushed past her and went into the dining-room and poured himself a shot of whisky and downed it in one gulp.

She didn't have time to remark on it however, for Oliver had just taken a sip of the wine she'd given him and held the glass back out to her.

'You wouldn't have anything drier, would you? I find this a bit cloying for my palate.'

'I'll look,' Samantha said quickly. Jason came back on to the deck with the whisky glass in his hand, and it was full again.

Samantha gave him a disapproving stare as she fetched a different wine for Oliver. Jason gave her a look that made chills run right down her spine. She'd seen it a few times before, but only when he was hovering at the net about to crush his opponent.

She chose to ignore it, knowing it was hopeless trying to jolly him out of it. Instead she turned back to Oliver. 'I'm delighted you've had such a successful summer and that the tour went well.'

Oliver leaned back, sipping his wine and nodding. 'Yes, it has been. I suppose you've had an "interesting" one yourself. What's it like traipsing all over after this . . . ball-player?'

Samantha bristled slightly, but shrugged it off. She knew how Oliver felt about things that weren't musical. She'd felt that way herself. But now . . .

'Very interesting, actually,' she said, prepared to tell him about it. 'They work incredibly hard. The conditioning, the stamina——'

'I'll bet.' Oliver's sarcasm was obvious, so she shut her mouth. A moment later she wished she'd opened it when Oliver took another sip of wine and asked, 'And so earthshakingly significant in its contribution to the human race—do you really make a living knocking around a stupid white ball, Cole?'

'I really do.' Jason's voice was deadly. It was the first thing he'd said in ages, and Samantha didn't like the sound of it at all.

'He's phenomenal,' she said to Oliver, deliberately ignoring his earlier sarcasm. 'You should watch him some time, Oliver. You wouldn't believe it.'

Oliver shook his head and laughed. 'I imagine you're right. But I'll just have to take your word for it, Sammie love. I really don't have the time.' He gave a faint shiver. 'Cooling off out here, isn't it? Do you suppose you could fetch my jacket?'

Samantha looked from Jason to Oliver, worried about what Jason might say if she left the two of them alone. But there was no help for it. 'Of—of course.'

When she came back, Jason gave her a look that was darker than ever. She gave him one in return.

He was the host, for heaven's sake. He was the one who had insisted she come home and had told Oliver he could come along. How dared he act as if everything was *her* fault?

'Thanks, sweetie, you're a pal.' Oliver shrugged on his jacket and leaned forward to plant a kiss on Samantha's cheek. 'I *should* have taken you along this summer.'

'I wondered when you'd realise.' Samantha was happy at last for a crumb of recognition. 'I really am as good as Nell.'

'Oh, not to play,' Oliver corrected blithely. 'To take care of me. I'm sure I need you more than Cole here does.'

'She doesn't take care of me,' Jason said quietly, his fingers wrapped around the whisky glass so tightly that his knuckles showed white with the strain.

Oliver got to his feet, giving Jason a disparaging smile. 'I should hope not. She has more sense than to get mixed up with your sort, Cole. But you could come with me now,' he said to Samantha, brightening as if a light had suddenly gone off in his head, 'especially since Ibañez has taken on Andrea. That was your one qualm, wasn't it? Teaching little Andi? Although what difference it would have made, I couldn't say. You were never much of a teacher anyway.'

Samantha stared, nonplussed. 'What?'

Oliver shrugged, leaning back against the railing, the breeze ruffling his silver blond hair into a nimbus around his angelic face as he smiled down at her. 'Well, I mean, you're hardly in Ibañez's league, my love. And——' he spread his hands wide '——you'll never be a soloist like your father. So it would be just as well if you did come with me after all.' He shrugged. 'Distraction be damned, you're worth it. We can get married if you want. I'll knock 'em dead with my music and you can cook my meals and wash my socks. How about it?' He gave Samantha a broad, smug grin.

Samantha opened her mouth to answer, but she never got a word out.

Jason said it all when he socked Oliver in the mouth.

CHAPTER TEN

'OH, MY goodness! Oliver! Are you all right? *Oliver?*'
Samantha flew at him, staunching the blood with the
hem of her dress.

Oliver, sagging back against the railing, looked dazed
and thunderstruck.

Samantha wiped the blood away, getting a glimpse of
the damage for the first time and wincing at the sight.
'Oh, Jason,' she wailed. 'How could you?'

'How could I?' His voice was coldly furious. He was
cradling his right fist in his left palm and looking as if
he'd like to do the same thing to her. Samantha winced
again and turned back to Oliver.

'We'll have to get him to Emergency.' As she spoke
she was already chivvying him down the stairs towards
the car.

'My mouff,' Oliver mumbled through his hand. 'He
hit my mouff.'

'It'll be all right,' Samantha soothed, patting his
shoulder.

'My mouff. My mouff. Wha' 'bout my confert?'

Oh, lord, the concert. Samantha didn't even want to
think about that! 'Get in. Call the hospital,' she said
over her shoulder to Jason. 'Tell them we're coming.'

He stared at her, unmoving.

She stopped and glared up at him. 'Don't just stand
there. Call them, for heaven's sake!'

But what good it would do, she didn't know. The
damage had already been done.

Oliver was not a good patient. Samantha supposed she shouldn't be surprised, and of course she couldn't really blame him. A split lip was no fun under any circumstances, and certainly not for a flautist with a concert the next afternoon.

'I can't play. I'll haff to canfel,' he muttered over and over again to Samantha all the way to Emergency, all through the stitching, and all the way back to his motel as the sun was beginning to come up on Sunday morning. 'I'll fue that baftard. I fwear I will.'

Samantha laid a hand on his arm. 'Now, Oliver, be reasonable.'

'Reavonable!' he yelped as he turned the key in the lock of the motel room door. 'I am pure reavon! That man iv a menaff. A fug. He fould be locked up.'

Samantha had had enough. 'No,' she said flatly, 'he shouldn't.'

Oliver looked at her, astonished. 'You can't be condoning it.' He stuck out his lip, giving her a good look at Jason's handiwork.

It was a beaut, but quite frankly he deserved it. 'In a manner of speaking, yes, I can.'

Oliver stared.

'He did it for me.'

There had never been a greater truth in her life than that. She had been mulling this astonishing fact over ever since she'd seen Jason's fist connect with Oliver's mouth. All the time she'd sat waiting for Oliver, she'd turned the notion this way and that, examining it, studying it, analysing it. And she had come to a very important conclusion: she really did matter to Jason Cole.

Jason the Easygoing, Jason the Mellow, Jason the Epitome-of-the-laidback-Southern-California-lifestyle never really exerted himself at all—except for the few things he cared about: volleyball, his father's company

and Andrea—whose motives she'd doubted, whose pro-
testations of love she'd ignored, had proved himself
firmly and irrevocably.

He cared about her. She might have doubted once,
but she doubted no longer. He hadn't hit Oliver for
himself, but for her. He was the first man in her life who
had put her ahead of himself. No one else had done
that—not Oliver, not Fritz, not even her father. He had
defended her; she was going to defend him, too.

'You were rude and obnoxious, Oliver.' She noted with
satisfaction that his jaw dropped at her words. 'You've
been rude and obnoxious before, but last night you
reached new heights. Or depths. Just what were you of-
fering me? A chance to be your slave?'

'Flave? Now wait a minute!'

'No. You wait. How dare you tell me I'm not much
of a teacher? If I hadn't been a good teacher, would
Andrea have got Ibañez to take her?'

'Well, I——'

'No, she wouldn't,' Samantha answered for him. 'I
am damned good at what I do. And I'm going to do it,
too. Regardless of what you think. Regardless of what
my father thinks.'

'Your favver——'

'My father is not God.' There, she had said it. Said
it to Oliver. Said it to herself. And, for once, believed
it. Because Jason had not only fought for her, he had
given her the courage to believe it. He had supported
her, had encouraged her, had given her confidence to be
her own person, not simply an extension of someone
else's.

'Thank you for your "offer", Oliver,' she said
scathingly, 'but there is no way on earth I would go with
you under any circumstances. I want more from my life
than that. It may not have been the wisest move in the

world for Jason to hit you, but quite frankly I'm glad he did.'

Oliver was looking at her as if he'd never seen her before. His eyes were positively boggling out of his head. 'You fink that jumped-up ape was juftified?'

'I think he appreciates me a damned sight more than you ever did.' Samantha met his gaze, her chin lifted, no longer the willing, submissive girl who'd bowed to his every wish and whim. 'You are a talented musician, Oliver, but you treat people—you treated me—like dirt.'

For a long moment neither of them said anything.

Then Oliver took a steadying breath. 'Well,' he said, his tone of calm deliberation belied only by the whiteness of his knuckles on the doorknob, 'Then we have nuffing more to fay to each ovver, do we, Famanfa?'

Samantha shook her head. 'No. I guess we don't.'

She had plenty to say to Jason, though. The car fairly flew along the narrow highway as she made her way back to Germaine's house. And, when she reached the driveway, she had the door open and was sprinting towards the house almost before the engine had died.

'Jason!' she shouted when she flung open the kitchen door, needing to tell him of her discovery, needing to throw her arms around him and tell him she loved him, needing—needing desperately—to make up for all that lost time. 'Jason!'

There was no answer.

She poked her head in the living-room, hoping to see him curled up on the sofa. He wasn't there. The clock read five forty-seven and she supposed he might have gone to bed. After all, he had a volleyball game at nine-thirty and he would need a bit of sleep. So she pounded up the stairs to the bedroom he and Toby were sharing and poked her head in. 'Jason?'

But only Toby lay sprawled on one of the single beds in the room. The other hadn't been slept in.

Blearily Toby opened an eye and stared at her. 'Wha's up?'

'Where's Jason?'

Toby shut his eyes again and his head dropped back against the pillow. ''S'gone.'

He'd left.

'Crisis at the plant,' Toby told her when he finally came awake enough to make sense. 'Said they called him in the middle of the night. I dunno what it was——' he shook his head '—but it musta been pretty serious for him to take off like that. We've gotta forfeit the game even.'

Samantha thought there was a possibility she might have forfeited the rest of her life.

'Where'd he go?'

Toby shrugged. 'Back to LA, I guess.'

But he hadn't. Samantha found that out when she, Andrea and Toby got there at last on Sunday night. She found the house empty and with no sign at all that Jason had ever returned.

'No, miss, he hasn't called in, let alone come to the office,' his secretary said when Samantha called her on Monday morning. 'I don't know where he is.'

No one did. Not Andrea. Not Toby. Not any of the board of directors of Cole Sportswear. No one.

'Where could he have gone?' Samantha threw herself down on to one of the chairs in the living-room, having exhausted all the possibilities for the hundredth time.

'And why?' Andrea added.

'I'll tell you why,' came an indignant voice from the other side of the screen door. 'Because the game is up!'

'Aunt Hortense!' Andrea leaped to her feet.

'Indeed.' Hortense clumped into the room and fixed Samantha with an accusing glare. 'And you are Ms Peabody.'

Samantha swallowed. 'Er—yes—but——'

Aunt Hortense snorted and poked Samantha's hair. 'No grey.'

'Er—no.'

She touched Samantha's NetWork T-shirt. 'No sloppy cardigan. No frowsy skirt.'

'Not any more. I——'

A plump finger prodded Samantha's freckled cheek. 'Not a wrinkle to be seen.' She eyed Samantha narrowly. 'Just how old are you, missy?'

Samantha could have wilted under the basilisk stare. 'T-twenty-four.'

'A child.'

Samantha bristled. She wasn't a child. Not now. Not ever again. And hearing the words made her trepidation disappear.

'I'm not,' she said stoutly. 'I'm a woman.' Jason had taught her that. 'And I'm a teacher.' He'd taught her that, too. 'A good one,' she added, 'or your friend Raul Ibañez wouldn't have taken Andrea on, would he?' She jutted out her chin and met Aunt Hortense's disapproving stare with an equally hard stare of her own.

For a moment Hortense didn't speak. Then she tossed her head. 'You're Ambrose Peabody's daughter,' she accused.

'Yes.'

'You didn't say so.'

'It wasn't important.'

Hortense's eyes widened. 'Not important?'

'Not to my teaching.'

'But——'

'I did a good job with Andrea, didn't I?'

'Well, yes,' Hortense conceded. 'But——'

'Then that's what matters.'

'About teaching maybe,' Hortense conceded. 'But you and Jason...' It didn't take a genius to figure out what she thought about that.

Samantha shook her head. 'There is no such thing as Jason and I.'

Aunt Hortense looked doubtful.

'But I wish there were.'

At that Aunt Hortense looked shocked. So did Andrea and Toby.

'I'd give anything if it were true,' Samantha told them stubbornly. She gave Hortense, Andrea and Toby a rueful smile. 'But I didn't trust him enough. And now he has no reason to trust me.'

'Well, I never! I——' Hortense stammered.

'You should have trusted him, too,' Samantha said flatly. 'You thought he was going to lead Andrea into a life of wild parties and frivolous flings. Nothing could be further from the truth. He cares about her. He wants her in his life because she's all the real family he has. Give him a break. Get angry at me if you must. But don't take this out on Jason. He deserves far better!'

Hortense was staring at her as if she couldn't believe her ears. So, for that matter, were Andrea and Toby.

This was a Samantha they hadn't seen before. This was a Samantha that Samantha had scarcely seen before. But this was a Samantha who knew what she wanted, who knew what she needed, and knew she had to go after it.

'What are you going to do?' Andrea asked her after Hortense had left.

'Yeah, what?' Toby wanted to know.

Samantha took a deep breath and sent a prayer winging to heaven. 'Find him.'

*   *   *

'If you want something, you have to go after it,' Jason had said to her the first week she had come. Samantha had always thought that a grasping sort of notion before—a 'take what you want' mentality of the sort that had deprived her of her mother.

But she began to see now that Louis could never have taken Margot if she hadn't wanted to go. And she also saw that Ambrose hadn't wanted her enough to go after her. He'd been content to let her leave because he had had a replacement waiting in the wings—Samantha. She had been a willing slave who'd felt guilty enough at her mother's defection to always want to please him, to always do his bidding.

But no more. She had become her own person this summer—thanks mostly to Jason Cole. He had done what she'd never dared to do for fear of losing her father's love: lived his life on his own terms.

Jason had rejected his father's notions of what he ought to be. He had worked for everything he had. But, when the chips had been down, he had come through in his own way to be a man of whom his father would have been proud.

It was what he'd encouraged her to do ever since she'd been here. She saw now that manipulation and acquiescence were not really love at all. Love was encouraging a person to become the best individual that particular person could be.

'Teach,' Jason had urged her. 'Why give it up? If it's what you want, go for it.'

She did want it. She would go for it, too. But more than that, Samantha wanted Jason. Now she had to find him. And convince him that she loved him, too.

It was Dena, of all people, who provided the key.

The other woman was clearly surprised to get Samantha's call. But Samantha had exhausted all other possibilities. Dena was the only person she hadn't asked, and she was desperate enough not to care.

If Jason had said that the other woman didn't figure in what he felt for Samantha, she had to believe him. She had, at least, to ask.

'You want to see Jason?' Dena sounded surprised.

'Yes. I—I need to talk to him.'

'Don't you think you've hurt him enough?'

'I—hurt him?' Samantha couldn't mask her astonishment.

There was a silence. 'He said you were going off with that—that musician.'

'You talked to him?'

'I——' Dena faltered. 'Oh, hell, he'll kill me if he finds out I told you.'

'Where is he?'

'Can't you just leave him alone?'

'No! Dena, please. I don't want to hurt him. I—I love him.' Dena was the last person Samantha had ever expected to be saying that to.

There was another silence now, longer than the first. It lasted so long that Samantha thought the connection might have been broken. 'Dena? Dena, did you hear what I said?' She was loath to repeat it. It made her sound such a fool.

'How could you leave him, then?' Dena demanded at last.

'I didn't leave him! I took Oliver to the hospital. When I came back, he was gone. Dena, I have to talk to him. Please! Where is he?'

'I don't—oh, heavens. Why do I get dragged into these things?' Dena wailed.

'Tell me,' Samantha commanded with every bit of firmness she could muster.

'Gibbs Island. Puget Sound. It's basically unin-habited, but he has a friend who owns a cabin there. He said he'd be back in a week or two. When he gets things sorted out.'

But Samantha wasn't waiting a week or two.

'You have to,' Dena said. 'You can't go there. It's remote. Inaccessible.'

'I'm going,' Samantha said determinedly. 'I'm going if I have to swim.'

So she did.

Puget Sound, even in August, was freezing. It was rough as well, a cold north wind blowing up just as she and the fisherman who'd agreed to take her set off.

'Be hard gettin' in with this weather,' he shouted over the roar of the engine and the slap of the waves. 'You could wait until tomorrow, see if the wind dies down.'

Samantha shook her head. She wasn't going to be deterred. It was already Thursday. The longer she waited, the greater her fears.

She had been cowardly most of her life, knuckling under to her father's wishes, bending to the slightest wind, never standing up for what she wanted, what she believed in. 'No!' she shouted back. 'I'm going now.'

But if Gibbs Island itself was any example of the hospitality she was going to encounter when she got there she was in for big trouble. One look at the chop of the waves and the narrow passageway into the only decent sheltered landing on the island, and the fisherman shook his head.

'Can't do it, lady. Too rough. Wreck my boat just tryin' to get in.'

'But you must!'

'Can't. Only a damn fool'd try to go through in this.'

'But——' She cast about for a miracle. 'Isn't there any way?'

'S'pose you could swim.' He grinned at the joke.

Samantha stared at the narrow strait, at the surging water. Her fingers clenched around the wooden rail. 'Could I?'

His grin vanished. 'Swim?'

'Yes.'

'You crazy, lady?'

'No.' But as she watched the swirling water, she wondered. 'I just have to get ashore.'

'You a good swimmer?'

'Passable.' That was, perhaps, a touch optimistic. Under Jason's watchful eye, she had learned, had practised, had progressed. She had swum with him every evening, had gained confidence, had, at last, done well. The surging waters off Southern California might not be the ragged pounding of a stormy Puget Sound, but the distance wasn't great. And she had desire on her side. And need. And love.

The fisherman gave her a long, hard look. 'You sure?'

Samantha stared at the shore, her eyes picking out the figure of a man, head bent, hands in pockets as he scuffed through the tide-line, his gaze caught for the moment by the boat just beyond the rocky line of the strait. Jason.

Her heart slammed against the wall of her chest. Could he see her? Would he want to? Did she dare give him a choice? 'I'm sure.'

The fisherman sucked in his breath. 'I'll bring you in close as I can.'

Stripping to her underwear, Samantha waited until he did, then plunged off the side and hit the water with a prayer.

It closed over her head, bone-chillingly cold and rough. She struggled to the surface and got slapped in the face by a wave. Tossing her head, she spat out the water, set her sights on the shoreline and blessed Jason for the gentle thoroughness of his teaching, which gave her courage now.

She squinted to see him, could barely pick him out when the rise and fall of the surf allowed it. No matter. He was there, standing, staring at the boat she'd just left. Determinedly, she struck out for shore.

She had never swum so far, never ached so badly. Each breath came as a searing flame in her lungs. Her heart pounded, her teeth ached, the blood thrummed loudly in her head. The shore seemed almost to recede with her every stroke.

At last she reached the strait, and there the force of the tide carried her forward. But, once inside the small natural harbour, she still had perhaps fifty yards to go.

The sea water stung her eyes and burned her throat. She ached, shivered, squinted and battled on. Another yard. Then another. Oh, lord, she could make it, couldn't she?

Yes, yes, her mind answered her. She could. She had to.

In the distance a rock-strewn, narrow sand beach beckoned. She couldn't see Jason any longer. But then, it had begun to rain and a man with sense would have gone inside.

Quite suddenly, just as she got in far enough to dare to grope for a toehold, there was a thrashing nearby and Samantha felt a new sort of panic. Not sharks, she prayed. Not in Puget Sound. At least, she'd never heard of any. Then what——?

'Samantha?' A sleek dark head surfaced almost next to her and she heard Jason's voice, hoarse with disbelief.

She very nearly sank with the shock of it. A pair of rough hands seized her. 'What in the hell do you think you're doing?' He was hauling her to shore even as he spoke.

Too tired to tell him she could do it herself, not even certain any longer that she could have, Samantha rested her head against him. 'Coming to you,' she said simply.

He sucked in an angry breath, took another half-dozen strokes, then stood up and began dragging her towards the sand. 'You damn fool, you could've been killed.'

She stumbled after him. 'N-no. I h-had a good teacher. The best.'

Jason muttered something under his breath that she couldn't hear. 'Come on,' he said gruffly and hauled her towards the cabin at the top of the hill.

She tried to stop, tried to talk to him, but he wouldn't listen. He just bullied her up the hill, into the cabin, into the bathroom.

'I'm all right,' she tried protesting through chattering teeth when he turned on the taps and stood glaring at her. 'I don't need a bath. I j-just had one. Give me a towel.' She needed to talk to him far more than she needed a hot bath.

'Strip,' he commanded. 'Or I'll do it for you.'

Samantha lifted her gaze and met his stormy one. A smile touched her mouth. She remembered the last time he'd said that to her. 'Go ahead.'

Jason stopped dead. 'What?'

'I said, go ahead.' Her smile widened as she dared him.

Jason scowled fiercely. His fists clenched and un-clenched. 'What the hell are you trying to do to me, anyway?'

'Do to you?'

He glared at her. 'You know I want you, Samantha. I've always wanted you. You don't have to prove it again. Unless this is some sort of torture. Is it? Flaunt yourself in front of the Neanderthal, then rejoin the love of your life?' He slammed his hand against the door-jamb. The mirror and the toothbrushes rattled.

Samantha just looked at him, aching for him, loving him, knowing now what he'd been thinking, hating herself for having done this to him. 'It's not that,' she said quietly.

'What is it, then?' His voice was bitter.

'Is it only that you "want" me?' Samantha asked him.

He turned a hard gaze on her. 'You want it all, don't you? What is this? My punishment for having dared lay a hand on God's gift?' He raked a hand through his wet, spiky hair. 'All right, damn it, I love you! There, is that what you came for?'

A heartbeat separated them. Then Samantha touched his cheek, leaving it there even though he winced and tried to brush her away.

'It's what I hoped for,' she breathed. 'It's the same thing I feel for you.'

She felt his jaw tremble. His eyelashes fluttered down, then jerked back up as he looked at her, first doubtfully, then with a flickering hope. 'What are you saying?'

'I'm saying that I love you, too.'

He shook his head slowly, then reached for her, taking her by the arms, holding her so that he could look directly into her eyes. 'I thought—I—What about... Oliver?'

'What about him?'

'You went with him.' She heard pain in his voice and understood now what he must have been thinking.

'I took him to get stitches. I told him a few home truths. Then I came home to you.'

Jason swallowed.

'You were gone.'

'Oh, lord,' he murmured.

'I love you,' Samantha said again, framing his face with her hands.

He shut his eyes. 'Oh, Sam.'

Hard arms went around her, hungry lips touched hers. His hands stroked her back, tangled in her hair, trembled violently as she returned the kiss with equal fervour.

At last, breathless, he leaned his forehead against hers. 'I shouldn't have done it. I shouldn't have hit him,' he said raggedly. 'After I had and you left with him, I thought it was the last straw. The final thing that would turn you against me. I was a Neanderthal for sure, just what you'd always said.'

'I'm glad you did it.'

Jason drew back, staring at her. 'You're what?'

'Glad. He deserved it.'

Jason made a sound that was half-sob, half-laugh. 'You like those Neanderthal tactics?'

Samantha touched her lips to his. 'They have their moments. It meant you cared.'

'Because I socked him in the mouth?'

'Because you showed me that I mattered.'

'Oh, yes, you matter!' He took her in his arms then, holding her against him, hard and deliberate. His mouth sought hers, burning, demanding. And Samantha gave everything she had to give.

They had the bath, but they took it together, Samantha at first shy, then gradually bolder, watching Jason, then touching him as he touched her, until finally he groaned and buried his face against her shoulder.

'We can't do this,' he muttered.

'Why not?' Samantha asked innocently. 'In books they do it all the time.'

'The first time we did it on the sand,' Jason answered, his voice unsteady. 'Not exactly the scenario I would have chosen.'

'It was wonderful,' Samantha protested.

He smiled. 'It was. And this will be too. I want it to be perfect for you.'

He dried her carefully, as if she were an exquisite piece of porcelain, then stood biting his lower lip while she insisted on returning the favour. At last, a thin sheen of perspiration already covering his body, he led her to his bed.

It was high and narrow, scarcely more than a camp bed, and he gave it a rueful glance. But Samantha touched his lips before he could speak. 'It doesn't matter. Nothing matters but you.'

And it didn't take him long to prove to her that he felt exactly the same way. Lovingly he stroked her, warming her with his hands and with his mouth and with the look in his eyes. And finally, when he parted her legs, she was almost frantic for the sense of completion.

'Jason! Now, please, now.'

'Now,' he agreed. And suddenly now was all there was.

Afterwards, when Samantha lay curled in the curve of his arm, tracing light patterns on his chest and wondering at the beauty and strength of this man who had seemed so unlikely to love her, she shook her head.

'What's wrong?'

'Nothing,' she replied. 'It just seems so unlikely—you and me.'

Jason stroked her hair. 'Yes.'

'You'd be more suited to Dena.' It was the last stumbling-block in her mind. Even though he'd protested that she didn't matter, even though Dena herself didn't seem to regard Jason as a boyfriend, it still hung there in Samantha's mind.

'The way you're more suited to Oliver?' Jason slanted a glance down at her.

'Oliver's a jerk. Dena's not.'

'No. But she's not for me.'

'You spent a lot of time with her.'

'Jealous?'

'Sort of,' Samantha admitted.

Jason rolled on to his side and smiled at her, though his eyes were serious. 'Dena and I go back a long way, and recently she's had some problems with her fast-lane life. She got into drugs pretty heavy. It can go with the territory if you let it. She got treatment and she's clean now. But a lot of people didn't want to take a chance on her again. So I had her do some ads for NetWork. She did well and she's got other offers now. I think she's on the right road. But——' he shrugged; almost embarrassed '—for a while she's needed a big brother. Somebody to talk to, to shore her up, have faith in her.'

Samantha, heart immeasurably lighter, touched his lips with hers. 'You are a wonderful big brother, Jason. You did the same for me. You gave me the courage to be myself.'

'I want to be more than your big brother,' he growled.

Samantha gave him a look of wide-eyed innocence. 'You do?'

'Yes, I do,' he mocked her tone as he dragged her on top of him. 'I want to be your friend, your lover, and your husband.' He framed her face with his hands. 'Will you marry me?'

Samantha smiled. 'Oh, yes.'

He paused. 'What will your father say?'

'Who cares? What will Aunt Hortense say?'

Jason grinned. 'Ditto.'

They loved again, then. For the rest of the evening and far into the night. And when the dawn came up Samantha put her arms around him and snuggled against him, replete, content, the happiest woman in the world.

She tilted her head so she could look up at him. He was looking back at her. 'Satisfied?' she asked softly.

Jason grinned. 'For the moment.'

But an hour later he drew her up on to his chest, and his hands began once more to stoke the fires within her. 'Play it again, Sam,' he whispered.

So she did.

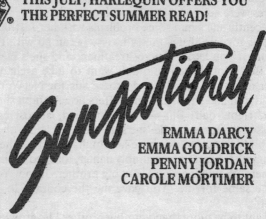

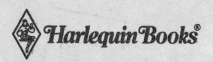
Harlequin Books®

GREAT NEWS...

HARLEQUIN UNVEILS NEW SHIPPING PLANS

For the convenience of customers, Harlequin has announced that Harlequin romances will now be available in stores at these convenient times each month*:

Harlequin Presents, American Romance, Historical, Intrigue:

> May titles: April 10
> June titles: May 8
> July titles: June 5
> August titles: July 10

Harlequin Romance, Superromance, Temptation, Regency Romance:

> May titles: April 24
> June titles: May 22
> July titles: June 19
> August titles: July 24

We hope this new schedule is convenient for you.

With only two trips each month to your local bookseller, you'll never miss any of your favorite authors!

*Please note: There may be slight variations in on-sale dates in your area due to differences in shipping and handling.

HDATES-R

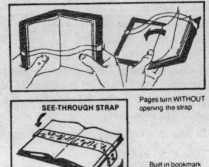

Back by Popular Demand

Janet Dailey
Americana

A romantic tour of America through fifty favorite Harlequin Presents® novels, each set in a different state researched by Janet and her husband, Bill. A journey of a lifetime in one cherished collection.

In June, don't miss the sultry states featured in:

Title # 9 - FLORIDA
        Southern Nights
   #10 - GEORGIA
        Night of the Cotillion

Available wherever
Harlequin books are sold.